11 STORIES

11 STORIES

CHRIS CANDER

Rubber Tree Press
Houston, Texas

 Published in the United States by Rubber Tree Press, Houston, Texas.

Library of Congress Control Number: 2013934292

Cander, Chris, 2013
11 stories / Chris Cander
p. cm.
ISBN 978-0-9889465-0-7

Printed in the United States of America
First Edition

10 9 8 7 6 5 4 3 2 1

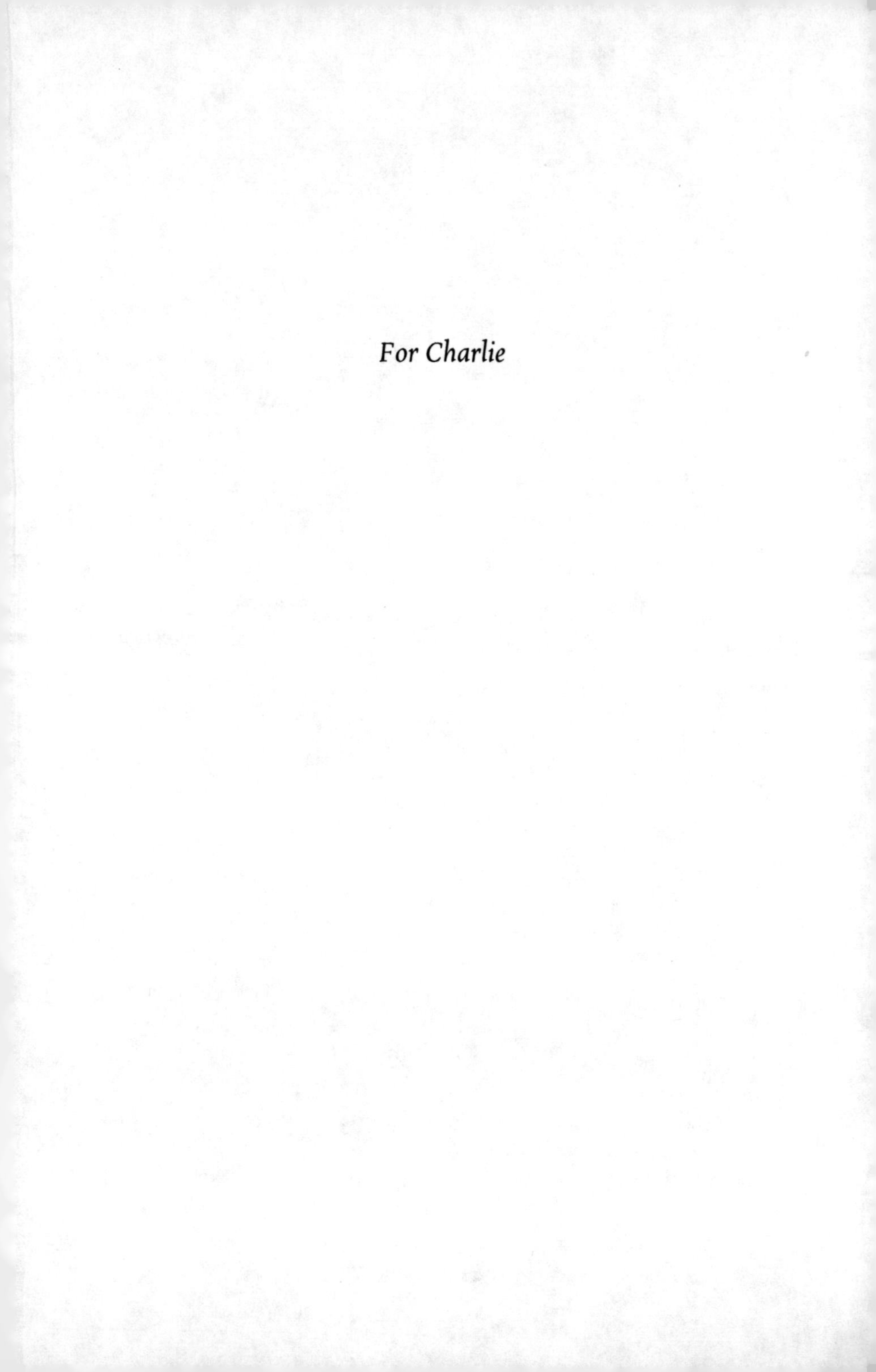

For Charlie

YESTERDAYS

It was a long way up for a sixty-seven-year-old man. He'd climbed those stairs nearly every day since he'd learned to walk; as a child toddling behind his mother, a boy with mischief in his bones, a young man seeking solitude. Mostly, though, he had climbed them as the superintendent of the building — both master and servant to the tenants who lived above him.

He used the steel-cage elevator sometimes, mostly to carry something heavy to the upper floors; a ladder, for example. His toolbox. Or if it was the end of a long day and someone buzzed for him, needing something urgently: a toilet was overflowing its unspeakable sludge, a boiler wasn't circulating, or in one resident's opinion another was making too much noise.

Once, he was roused from his basement office (really just a small room that fronted his modest living quarters behind the laundry room) because a bird that turned out to be a black-crowned night heron, probably from the nature sanctuary a few blocks south, had inexplicably flown into one of the windows on the tenth floor. It didn't quite break the glass, but it unnerved the spinster who'd been sitting in the seat beneath it reading the book of Revelation and smoking something that smelled a lot like marijuana. After Roscoe had taped the window and promised he'd have the whole thing changed in the morning, he'd had to sit down on the edge of her plastic-covered sofa until she was calm enough to allow his leave.

Afterward, he'd carried a box down to the sidewalk beneath her window, wrapped the broken bird in an old towel and taken it back to his quarters. He could have incinerated it the way he did all the rest of the flotsam and jetsam the tenants deemed trash, but he felt sorry for it in that moment of darkness. So he laid the box on the floor of his living room and said a prayer he could remember his mother saying at the funerals of his uncles, one by one; his grandmother; a distant cousin; and of course, his father. "We thank you for his life and his death, for the rest in God he now enjoys, for the glory we shall share evermore at your right hand, in Jesus's name. Amen." It was the first time he'd ever said a prayer on his own. Even sitting in the front pew at his mother's funeral in the spring of '64, when he was only twenty—just two years after burying his father — he'd had no words to pray. Instead, in the nightclub of his mind, he'd heard the lyrics of Chet Baker's ironic, iconic, "I Get Along Without You Very Well." But that's how he was. Words came uneasily from his mouth, but not music. Music fell freely.

He was tired by the time he opened the door to the roof, but once he stepped out onto the terrace his fatigue dissipated. It was one of those unseasonably warm October evenings. The dry breeze lifted people's spirits and windows and inspired them to spill out onto the streets, pushing baby strollers and following dogs from one hydrant to another with blithe patience or taking early dinners alfresco at any of the countless cafés with their folding chairs and tables. Irish pubs flung open their windows and the Italian grocer set up a table outside his shop with pumpkins and pomegranates. Roscoe let the door shut behind him and stood on the roof, his old Blessing Standard trumpet dangling from the loose grip of the hand that still had all five long, slender fingers. He tipped his head back, closed his eyes, and filled his lungs with the crisp, pinked, sunset air that mingled with the exhaust from the compactor room.

Several years before, some of the tenants had started a community garden. There were five rows of planter boxes, each of them six feet long and two wide, bursting with herbs and squash and other small crops. He walked past but then stopped, triggered by something, and went back to the first box. He bent down and relieved the top of one woody rosemary stem of its spikey leaves, rolled them between his fingers and held the tips to his nose. He'd always loved rosemary. The smell of it reminded him of something that seemed just out of reach, some memory or reality to which he wasn't quite entitled but yearned for all the same. He dropped the bruised leaves and continued.

The corner of the roof where the south and east faces met wasn't really a corner at all. It was round and stood out several feet beyond the main structure like a turret. He had to climb over a short wall to get out to the curved edge, but even with that minor inconvenience he never could understand why he was always alone up there. Why everyone didn't climb out and lean against the precipice to watch the sun come up over the lake's horizon or just to get a sense of perspective, to look down at things and realize how small they really were. When he was young, he'd passed many hours tucked behind the cornice, its lion's heads lined up beneath his own like a row of personal guards. It had been a good place to hide from his father, who knew the building almost as well as Roscoe did. His father never did discover him crouching behind that little parapet, sitting out a scolding or waiting for a mood to pass. Roscoe practiced the trumpet there, too, because he could blow into the wind and his notes would get carried away without anybody hearing, especially during those difficult years when he had to learn a new way of fingering the valves.

But this evening, with its perfect sunset and clear, dry sky, Roscoe Jones wasn't going out to hide. There was nobody to hide from; everyone that mattered was gone.

This evening, he was seeking.

He lifted first one creaky, aching leg over the small dividing wall and then the other, and walked up to the curved and sloping edge. He stood there, pressing his old-man belly against the terra cotta for a moment, gathering his strength, and then hoisted himself up onto the flat ledge, careful not to lose his footing or drop his trumpet, because that would have ruined everything.

Once his feet were under him, he stood slowly up to his full and impressive height and without closing his eyes or moving his mouth he said the second prayer of his adult life, which was actually more like a wish. Then he took a deep breath and looked out from this strange elevation at the world below and beyond. It was like being a preacher behind a pulpit, waiting for the faithful to settle down before beginning the sermon, or an actor on a thrust stage, waiting for the spotlight to illuminate the scene. He stood there holding his trumpet, and when he was ready, he brought it to his lips.

All it took to steady his knees from their tremble, standing exposed as he was at such a great height and with all the world to see him, was that landing of the mouthpiece against his lips. Gentle and familiar as a kiss from a long-loved woman, the horn on his face let him fall into the deepest part of himself, forgetting the void, the lack, the lonesomeness. When he buzzed his lips and blew his own breath through the purification system of the trumpet, it was distilled into something far greater than him; his exhales suddenly had purpose and meaning, translated as they were into rich, pure song.

Roscoe knew early on he was going to make music. When he was a boy of eight or nine years old, slipping away as he often did from his father's glare, he started hanging around the back entrance of the jazz club near his building. He'd found that when he got tired of walking, he could sit against the brick wall and listen to the strains of music whenever someone went through the door. It wasn't too long before the owner took pity on his rapturous face and let him come inside to listen, and not too long after that he was allowed to come in whenever he liked, even without knocking — and then, after he took a broom from its lean against the wall and started sweeping up cigarette butts from backstage, he was earning a nickel here and there, a pat on his curly, dark hair, and the right to watch the sessions from the wings. Only one waitress, a girl around twenty with a child of her own at home, seemed concerned by his ever-presence. But the owner just laughed and swatted her on the fanny and told her to mind her own business, the boy was just fine.

One night, a famous trumpeter by the name of Clifford Brown came to play. He showed up in a black suit, sweating a little where his neck strained against his tie in spite of the December cold, and laughing at something his piano-player had said. Roscoe watched as they set up and warmed up, and by the time they'd finished their first set he didn't want to take another breath if he couldn't blow it through a shiny brass trumpet.

The quintet took a break, and Roscoe watched as Clifford carried his trumpet backstage and laid it carefully in its case before he went to find the men's room. When they'd all gone to wherever it was they went for the fifteen minutes, Roscoe crept out of the shadows and opened the case and held the instrument in his none-too-clean hands. Then, turning his back to the door, he brought it to his mouth the way he'd seen Clifford do, and blew. It was like blowing a balloon. He produced no sound but his own sputtering breath, even as he tried again and again. Finally, he moved his mouth a certain way, closing his lips tighter against the mouthpiece, and he managed to push a note through the pipe, flat and burbling, like something out of the wrong end of a dog. Encouraged, he blew until he was light-headed and heaving for air, achieving a decent sound only once. Then from behind, he heard someone laugh. He spun around and there was Clifford Brown, with his hands in his pockets and his belly jiggling.

"Hey Brownie, you gonna let that kid spit on your horn like that?" said the drummer, Max, who'd come up behind.

"He's not gonna hurt it," Clifford said. He walked over to Roscoe, whose light brown face had gone red, and whose reed-thin body wasn't quite able to hide the trumpet that he'd stashed behind his back. "You trying to upstage me or something?" Clifford said, putting his hands on his hips, looking pretend-serious.

"No sir." Even his own shame couldn't keep Roscoe from staring up at the man who'd made such magic onstage. When Clifford held out his hand, Roscoe's shoulders fell. He sighed and placed the trumpet into it. "Sorry," he muttered, and hung his head. He turned to go, already mourning his banishment from the club that had become his refuge.

"Come on now. No reason to slink off like that. Come back here a minute." Roscoe turned around. "Max, you seen my other case?" Clifford said.

"You're kidding me," Max said, but he handed it to Clifford, shaking his head the whole time.

"Here it is. Now come here, little man, and let me show you something."

That was fifty-seven years and one middle finger ago. He'd found somebody to teach him the basics, and he'd practiced nearly every day since on Clifford Brown's hand-me-down Blessing. He'd even turned out to be what some people called a prodigy. His father never did approve, said that he didn't like that washed-out look he got on his face when he played, but eventually, reluctantly, even he had to admit that Roscoe had a gift. He never would tell that to Roscoe directly, nor would he condone the hours Roscoe spent locked in his room or hidden god-knew-where, practicing. He didn't go to the club the first night Roscoe sat in with a local tenor saxophonist when he was just fourteen years old, nor was he there ten months later, the night that would be Roscoe's last to play in public — until, that is, tonight.

Roscoe settled his fingers on the valves. After so long, he could hardly remember what it felt like to use his middle finger — or even to have one — but he considered it briefly, wondered what people would think if they could see his hand now, working the valves like he'd never gotten his hand stuck in the iron grip of the cage elevator, like he hadn't spent years building up the strength in his pinkie and teaching his ring finger to move independently and figuring out how to keep the galling stump out of the way. Even now he suffered a moment of anger and shame, thinking of those lost years. He'd lost more than just a finger. Far more. Then again, he'd gained something, too.

But by the time he played the first three notes of "Yesterdays," none of it mattered. He started slow, sustaining the lower notes, feeling the melancholy mood emerge. He didn't so much feel it as float around it. Even as his lips and fingers did their work, his soul slipped his body and hovered somewhere close by, tethered only by his breath, flapping like a flag on the wind of the ascending scale and urgently straining for freedom against its fetter when he held the pitches in the upper range.

If he could have embodied himself while he was playing, he might have noticed that the people down below had stopped their strolling and chatting and eating and were now looking more than a hundred and forty feet up at the precipice stage upon which Roscoe stood. Tilt-headed curiosity first, their ears not accustomed to hearing music from such a direction; then alarm — they grasped one another's arms, widened their eyes at each other, gathered unconsciously into tighter groups, look how high up he is! How close to the edge! — then as Roscoe continued to play without falling, simplifying the circle-of-fifths progression with a slow, reflective tempo, they let themselves relax somewhat and return to curiosity, or even move past it to appreciation.

Windows opened beneath him, and people looked around for the source. It seemed to come from everywhere and nowhere at the same time, mingled as it was with the sounds of street traffic and the machinery of urban dwellings. But because the air was dry, "Yesterdays" cut through it more clearly than it otherwise would have, and by the time Roscoe was descending chromatically through the final melodic phrases — G, F, C, D, E, and E, E, E — there was an audience of fifty people at least, or a hundred, or maybe more.

He held that last E as long as he could, until his breath was nearly gone, and then his soul slammed back into his old body so hard it seemed to jostle him a little, and he became aware of the sound of clapping and even a few whistles which grew louder but didn't displace the purity of that last E. A gentle wind off the lake picked up and lifted the hem of his untucked shirt. He closed his hand around his trumpet and held it against his belly, then he looked out, below and then beyond. There were people clapping, calling for an encore. He hadn't expected that. He searched the crowd for faces that he knew, but from such a distance, nobody was distinct. But then again, even up close, it was often hard to tell who people were. It would've been nice to recognize someone, he thought, as he prepared himself to bow. One someone, in particular. It would've been really nice. But maybe it didn't matter; they were all just people living their lives, sharing an unforeseen moment, congregating on some distant future memory, and now they were clapping for him, as though they knew him, as though he were somebody worth knowing. Maybe he was, and maybe they were too, and it was that thought — along with the E still singing in his ears — that occupied his mind as he folded himself in a deep and grateful bow ... and fell.

11

If someone were standing inside the building, say, at the wall of brass mail slots, or else near the reception desk close to the heavy glass front doors, and happened to be looking at the elevator when the operator slid closed the steel cage door with a certain well-hefted slam, that clanging impact would box his ears at the exact same instant he saw the latch close. But if he were to stop for a moment, and look up from his mail or away from the pretty receptionist, he might think about the fact that the sound of the cage closing should actually have come just infinitesimally slightly after the sight, since the speed of sound is considerably slower than the speed of light. But the brain doesn't notice such everyday lags such as this, and besides, there are other things worth considering (the pile of mail, the pretty girl) and as such, the elevator begins to rise and nobody stops to consider the flexibility of time.

But if one is falling, well, that's a different story.

Roscoe became aware of the fall the instant his feet, still shod in their daily polished loafers, lifted off the tarmac of the building and his body levitated in that singular but inevitably compromised verticality just inches below and away from the Jasper granite shelf upon which he'd been standing. But the awareness didn't translate immediately into fatality. Instead, it led to a protracted and unwinding retrospection.

There was a moment — a few millimeters' worth — of incredulity before his mind shattered into countless individual memories all called up for equal consideration. The quotidian alongside the exceptional. He felt an absence of panic, an absence of rush. In fact, despite his physical acceleration of roughly thirty-two feet per second per second, it seemed a slothful fall. Within this horizon moment of suspension, Roscoe seemed to possess an infinite capacity to review his bygone experiences — and there seemed to be infinite experiences and thoughts and emotions all coexisting in the eternity of his fall.

They might have competed, those countless memories, for superiority via some hierarchy of importance or relevance, but instead, as Roscoe began his battle with gravity, they organized themselves in a bizarrely logical descending order. Resting upon nothing, as bottomless and bankless as a waterfall, Roscoe's life narrative shattered into droplets; a moving, living flow organized not by chronology, but bound by a vertical unity like an elevator descending in its shaft — starting with the last time he had entered the penthouse belonging to the award-winning author Lenny Dreyfus.

The call had come from the woman who lived directly beneath Lenny's apartment. There was a leak, she'd said, from the ceiling above her bathtub, which meant, of course, that it was coming from the penthouse. Roscoe had knocked, and waited, and knocked again. It wasn't his business to know the comings and goings of the tenants, but the mere fact of his living among them made him privy to their habits. He knew Lenny didn't often go out in the afternoons, and so he knocked again. When

Roscoe's cell phone rang (a kindergarten teacher on the fourth floor had helped him set Miles Davis's "No Blues" as his ringtone) and the leak-ee wanted to know if the leak had been found, he finally shuffled through the forty-nine keys he carried and opened the door.

It wasn't his business to know the scents inside the tenant's apartments, either, but the fact of his having to come and go for regular and sundry reasons established an olfactory intimacy that he'd have preferred not to have. Had he been blindfolded, he'd have known Lenny's apartment simply by the manifest smell of new and old books: sharp ink and mushrooms, vanilla and mildew, leather and wood. It permeated all 3,154 square feet, as it had since the day the man had moved in some twenty years before. That scent was stronger than either of Lenny's two marriages: the first to a sparkling young dancer who left him for a playwright eighteen months later and the second, which lasted nearly sixteen years, produced no children except for his six novels and had ended only a few weeks before the leak occurred.

"Mr. Dreyfus," Roscoe said into the book-smell. His voice was quiet; he didn't care much for interacting. He hoped nobody was home and he could go on and fix the leak and then return to his basement and his trumpet. He walked tentatively inside. Walls of windows permitted a kind of inspired schoolroom light. "Mr. Dreyfus?" There was a spill of mail on the table in the foyer. Roscoe squinted at it; the first in the stack was an exotic travel brochure addressed to Dr. Jennifer Dreyfus.

"Mr. Dreyfus?"

Roscoe knew he should go straight to the bathroom and address the problem of the leak, but he was always troubled by entering a tenant's home when they weren't present. He was aware of the standard prejudice against his color, even though it was so light that back when he'd been young and hanging around the club, people murmured opinions about his being able to "pass."

"Mr. Dreyfus?" He put a hand to his keys to keep them from jangling and veered to the left, past the chef's kitchen that had been designed for entertaining but had been used only once or twice in the past decade for anything other than carryout. Past the living room with the high-pile rug and leather-and-chrome chairs and the tasteful bookshelves with artfully placed objects. Roscoe knew that water was dripping from somewhere and it was his job to find and fix it, but now that he was there, he wanted to stand by the window of Lenny Dreyfus's office and look down.

It had been months, maybe a year, since Roscoe had been called to the penthouse; the last time, Dr. Dreyfus had still been present, hovering and compulsive in her attention to detail. She'd seen a mouse coming from her husband's office, and would Roscoe please attend to it immediately. Lenny, hunched and somber, wearing sunglasses despite the dim, had hardly looked up from his electric typewriter when Roscoe went in. A typewriter. Even Roscoe, who wanted no part of modern technology and who only used a cell phone because the property owner insisted, found that hard to understand. Roscoe had gone quietly in, his footsteps muted behind the key-clacks, searching for a mouse or the hole from which it had come, but when he'd seen the bank of south- and east-facing windows and the almost cartoonish sunset matting the skyline beyond them, he'd forgotten himself. It looked more magical somehow through Lenny's tinted windows than it did even from the roof. How, with a view like that, he wondered, could anybody be anything but joyful? Of course one had to be able to see to enjoy the view and for the past year or so, though he wouldn't admit it, Lenny had been slowly going blind.

"Get the fuck out!" Lenny had yelled, all of a sudden. "Get the FUCK out of my office!"

Roscoe felt himself blanch, leaving a cold damp on his face and neck. He turned away from the beauty beyond the windows and ducked his head as he moved past Mr. Dreyfus, who had pushed himself away from his desk and was slapping his hand against the top.

"Get the fuck out of here!"

"I'm sorry, Mr. Dreyfus," Roscoe said as he passed.

"What? What's that? Who's there?" He blinked wildly behind his glasses, and held aloft a weapon of rolled-up newspaper. "That you, Roscoe? Fuck, I thought you were that rat my wife's been sniveling about."

"I didn't mean to interrupt your work," Roscoe said. "I just came in to set a trap. Didn't mean to upset you."

"Oh hell, you didn't upset me." Lenny sighed

and dropped back down into his swivel desk chair. He took off his glasses and pinched together the etched lines between his eyebrows. "Nor did you interrupt my work, as I can't seem to get a decent fucking thing done." He slapped his newspaper sword onto the floor, which unfurled its sheaves on the way down and landed with hardly a thud. "Send my wife in when you're finished, will you? That is if she's not *indisposed*. Fine job I did taming the shrew."

Lenny's office looked different the night Roscoe went up to solve the leak. An unmade cot took up space in front of the bookshelves, the sheets rank and twisted like someone had sweated through many nightmared sleeps beneath them. The desk was a wreck of papers, the wastebasket overflowing with crumpled wads — not even a week's worth, because Lenny's housekeeper came every Monday and Friday. The typewriter was on and purring, but the loaded sheet was blank. "Mr. Dreyfus?" Roscoe whispered as he stepped over a pile of magazines, but he wasn't looking for him, not yet, not really. He stepped up to the south-facing floor-to-ceiling window and looked out at the moonlight sparkling on Lake Michigan.

Roscoe stood with his hands folded behind his back, letting his mind drift until a gust smacked the glass hard enough to startle him from his reverie and make him remember the leak. He sighed and turned his back on the glass. Passing Lenny's desk, he stopped to turn off the typewriter and noticed that the sheet locked inside wasn't blank after all. There was one line in the middle of the page that said, "Does it ever get any fucking easier?"

With few exceptions, Roscoe had never stolen anything. But after only a brief hesitation, he unrolled the paper out of Lenny's typewriter, folded it twice and shoved it into the pocket behind his ring of keys. Then he went into the bathroom, where he found the author passed out but alive in his claw-foot bathtub, an inch of water covering the tile floor.

Roscoe struggled with the heft of Lenny's aging, water-logged body as he tried unsuccessfully to get him out of the tub. Lenny was splayed out and pruned, his belly lumpy-round and marked by six decades of wear, his pale skin constellated with moles of various shapes and colors. Roscoe had never been so close to a naked man, and the disgust he felt by the proximity was overshadowed only by his duty not just to a fellow man, but to a tenant. He was only a year younger than Lenny, and he wondered as he gripped him beneath the flabby arms: was his own midsection such a paunch? Were his own legs so stringy? At what point did age begin to corrode the body so visibly, even as its owner ignored the claim? Roscoe, unable to get Lenny to his feet, let him back down. He tried not to note Lenny's flaccid penis, which floated between his nearly hairless legs like a soggy mushroom, as he reached between the man's ankles to drain the water.

Lenny coughed.

"You all right, Mr. Dreyfus?"

Lenny looked in Roscoe's direction from behind the sunglasses he wore even then, and smacked his lips.

"That you, Roscoe?"

Roscoe stood up and shoved his hands into his pockets. He felt the sharp, folded edges of the stolen aphorism. Water burbled down the drain.

"Yessir."

Lenny smiled vaguely and dropped his head back against the edge of the tub. He closed his eyes for a moment and Roscoe thought he'd passed back out, but just as the water level dropped below his hips, he seized up from the cold. "Towel," he said, and Roscoe handed him one, a thick Egyptian cotton the color of eggplant, monogrammed in gold thread. Lenny spread it inelegantly over himself as the water drained, and when Roscoe leaned down to help cover him more fully, Lenny shooed him off.

Then he laughed. "You ever read *Narcissus and Goldmund*?" he said.

Roscoe blinked slowly, watching the last of the water — filthy with human taint — get sucked down into the bowels of the building the way liquid would go through a human being. He kept his eyes off the bloated lump beneath the fancy towel, and scratched the back of his head with the index finger of his compromised hand.

"Really? Hermann Hesse?" Lenny said, and he slid down a little deeper into the tub and looked up blindly at Roscoe. He nodded at something then pointed a trembling finger. "You're Narcissus," he said. "And I'm Goldmund. You should read it, Roscoe, you really should. It's about us." Lenny pointed from Roscoe to himself, then, as though tired from the effort, closed his eyes. A moment later, he spoke again. "You. You are Narcissus." His eyes rolled behind his glasses. "You're the ascetic. You're disciplined and self-controlled. You do your work on the boilers and the elevator and the rat-traps and you stand there with your shoulders back like a soldier, noble and forthright. Aren't you, Roscoe? Aren't you noble and forthright?" Lenny laughed, and his ugly belly shook beneath the towel. "I bet you are," he said. "But I, I am Goldmund. The artist. And my free, abiding spirit renounces all things orderly and controlled. I am a writer. A writer, Roscoe! Do you have any idea what that means? An idea hits me and my routine is abandoned to it, my discipline goes only to my work. My freedom is lost to my soul."

Lenny coughed again, and drew up his thin knees.

"I'm a hard-working Goldmund. As long as my task fascinates me, I'll work like a zealot," he said. "Fucking shame my 'best' work is a farce. Did you know that, Roscoe? Did you know that the fucking National Book Award I got was a fucking joke? I'll tell you a secret. I only wrote that fucking book because nobody took my other work seriously. So I figured out what would make the prize committees cum in their pants, and I wrote *that.* And they bought it! Can you believe it?" He laughed, but it came out like a cough, and Roscoe reached down to help him up from his fragile position, naked in a damp bathtub, but Lenny just swatted the air and curled himself into a more comfortable position. "Don't fuck with me, Roscoe," he said.

"You should get out of the bathtub."

"When I'm goddamned ready to I certainly will."

"The water's leaking through Ms. Freeman's ceiling. I need to get this cleaned up."

"Sylvia Freeman. That woman's probably never read a book in her life. Crazy as bat shit, that one," Lenny said, and he pushed his sunglasses higher up on his squat nose. "She can wait a goddamned minute. I'm in the middle of a confession here, Roscoe."

Roscoe wondered briefly if Lenny would have a problem with him using the monogrammed towels to mop up the spilled water, but decided that if he were going to be held captive as a drunk old man's confessor, he could use anything he pleased.

"I don't have much time left," Lenny said, his voice suddenly low. The syntax was that of a statement, but the intonation curled up slightly at the end, like a question, like a plea. Then, as though Roscoe had replied, Lenny continued, somewhat more indignant. "Because I can't see worth a fuck, that's why, and because I'm old. I'm rotting. And you, Narcissus. You've got to be nearly the same age as me. Why do you look so hearty and hale? Look at you. You've still got hair, hardly gray. Only a little thick at the waist. Is that what being peaceful does to an old man? Huh, Narcissus? Are you at peace?"

Roscoe looked at Lenny, who was starting to shiver. His blanched skin was mottled with goose bumps. Roscoe dragged the pile of fancy, plush towels around the tile floor with his foot. Was he at peace? His finger itched, as it sometimes did. The one that had dropped onto the polished marble floor sixty years before, tentacles of nerves and sinew draining the blood that had been circulating through it just seconds before the elevator gate closed on it. His finger itched, but it wasn't there. And there were the other voids, the ones that itched more than a missing finger. No. He wasn't at peace.

"Maybe nobody gives a fuck anymore. Maybe I

should just be happy with my ill-gotten gains and drift off into an appropriate obscurity. But I can't help it, see? I'm an artist! I have things to say! But you know what? I can't get past knowing that nobody wants to read what I have to say. They all want that gimmicky shit I wrote when I wanted to prove that I was worthy of notice. Nobody wants a *quiet* novel, I'm told. 'Quiet!' What the fuck does that even mean? Do you know what it means, Roscoe?"

Roscoe shook his head, and tossed down another few dry towels. Why did one person have so many towels?

"I've got so little time left," Lenny said again, and he reached out of the tub and dragged a heavy, sopping towel back in to cover more of himself. "I'm a lonely old man. There, I admitted it. I'm alone and blind and my work is pointless. And you want to know something else? I'll tell you. All those readings I gave, all those interviews, the book tours. I'll admit it: I used to plan beforehand the few little erudite quotes I'd drop in whenever I answered a question. You know, I'd pause for a moment and look up and to the right of the audience like I was searching through my vast mental library for just the right line, and then I'd say something like, 'As the great so-and-so once said ...' and everyone in the audience would nod like they knew what the fuck I was saying, which of course they didn't, not all of them anyway. We were all there posing for each other, the learned and the desperate. Do you know which one was which, Narcissus?

"I didn't want people to know what I didn't really know. Hell, I didn't even read half the books that writers are supposed to not only read but to *cherish*. Want to know something? I never read *Moby Dick*. Or *Huckleberry Finn* or *Crime and Punishment* or *The Trial*. The list of books from which I should be able to pull meaningful quotes to enrich my conversations is a hell of a lot longer than the list of books from which I can. A hell of a lot longer. Maybe that's where I fucked up. Maybe," Lenny said, rattling under the wet towels. Then he looked up through his glasses at Roscoe like a mole peering through a sky-lit tunnel and said, "Narcissus, I'm telling you, you're a lucky son of a bitch. You really are."

Roscoe stopped his swabbing.

Lenny continued. "Your life is laid out for you. People know what to expect from you. They know what you are, what you do. The problems that need fixing — the toilets and the boiler and the elevator shaft — you fix them. Done. Everybody's happy. You're the monk, the abbot. You don't have to worry about the lush needs of women, or the demands of a fickle reading public. All you have to do is wake up, do your job, and you're done. I envy you, Narcissus, I really do. Now help me up. The water's all gone out of this fucking tub. There's a leak, I believe you said. Fucking thing. Better have a look at it."

He extended his pruned hand and let Roscoe heave him to his feet where he wobbled for a moment. "Hand me a dry towel, will you?" he said.

Roscoe opened first one cabinet and then the rest. "There aren't any more dry ones," he said.

"What do you mean? There's at least a dozen in here. I just had them monogrammed." Holding onto the sink, Lenny stepped out of the tub. After his foot landed with a squish, he looked down. "Jesus fucking Christ, Roscoe! Are those my new towels on the floor? Are you standing on my new fucking towels?"

"Sorry, Mr. Dreyfus. I was trying to sop up the water you spilled."

"I spilled? Jesus Christ, Roscoe, you said yourself there was a leak. That's *your* job, abbot. Who trains you people anyway? Don't you have better sense than to use brand fucking new towels that cost more than you probably make in a week? I should report you to someone. The fucking Better Sense Bureau. Now find me a goddamned dry towel before I freeze to death standing here in your fucking mess!"

Roscoe managed to get Lenny back to his office, into a dry set of pajamas, and settled onto his cot like a child — a child who muttered and cussed and damned the world of women and words and service personnel until he fell into a drunken sleep. Then Roscoe cleaned the floor and took the towels down to his own apartment to launder.

There, he took an old picture frame he had and removed the signed photograph inside. He unfolded the paper he'd taken from Lenny's typewriter and smoothed it out with the flat of his hand, then put it where the photograph had been. He hung the frame back on the wall, above his nightstand where it had hung for the last few decades at least, and stood back to look at it with his thumbs hooked into the pockets of his pants.

Does it ever get any fucking easier?

When the towels were dry, Roscoe folded them as precisely as any ascetic would, with all the gilded initials facing the same direction. He had them back in the bathroom before Lenny had even begun to sweat out the scotch.

10

There was something disturbing about Sylvia Freeman's window. It had always been that way, inside as well as out. It was the only one in the building that wasn't shuttered, hung with attractive treatments or left open to the view and to voyeurs, if they were so inclined. No, Sylvia had long ago tacked up sheets and towels and even, on one window, a shower curtain covered in rubber ducks. Anything, it seemed, to hide the hoarding.

Roscoe's domino game of memory stopped on the tile of the day that Sylvia had gone down to his apartment, something she'd never done before and only one other time since, and rapped accusingly on the door.

"You were in my apartment yesterday, were you not?" she said when he opened it. He'd been cleaning his trumpet in the bathtub; all the parts save the felt were soaking in a mild solution.

"Good afternoon, Mrs. Freeman," he'd said, smiling with his mouth only.

"Were you not?" She stood with her hands on her bony hips, her dark eyes narrowed beneath a pair of riotous eyebrows and skin so deeply lined that she looked at least a decade older than her thirty-five years. Her dark hair was thinning beyond her forehead, and despite her tidy attire she bore the faint, unpleasant odor of steamed broccoli and sour carpet and unwashed hair. "I saw the notice you posted by the mailboxes that you were going to be going into our apartments."

He wiped his hands on the towel he was holding, and thought back to the previous day. The Freon he'd added to the compressor, the barking dog on six he'd had to ask the tenant to quiet down, the meeting with the building owner who was organizing a tour of restoration architects and another for the United States Secretary of the Interior, who was considering the building for a national landmark designation. And yes, there'd be no forgetting Sylvia's apartment. He'd gone down to fumigate because the surrounding tenants had been complaining not only of the odd smells coming from her unit, but also the cockroaches, which theretofore hadn't been a problem if they'd even been there at all.

"Yes ma'am, I believe so," he said. "Are you still seeing any bugs? I sprayed the whole building. Must've been all the rain we got last couple weeks."

"No, Roscoe, that's not the problem. I seem to be missing a very important box of paperwork, and I wonder if you happen to know where it might be."

Even now, he could remember the interior of her apartment with painful detail. The smallish kitchen had lost all function except as a repository for hundreds of bottles of spices and gadgets and unwashed dishes and boxes of expired pantry goods and empty soda cans and plastic cups and bags. The sink was filled with cookbooks; the refrigerator had been unplugged and the rotted food in it was unrecognizable and far beyond even emitting odor. Newspapers were stacked everywhere and a shoebox of coupons was tilted like a precarious cherry on top of the piles. He hadn't known where to begin with the insecticide; nothing less than a fire would indemnify the place from an infestation.

The kitchen, impossibly, wasn't even the worst part of the house. Sylvia had only lived there for about three years; her husband, an accountant, had died of an aneurysm exactly a week after they'd moved in, at the age of thirty-four, before the boxes had even been unpacked. Roscoe remembered seeing her coming in and out of the foyer back then, petite and neat and smiling, touching her husband on the small of his back, giving him endearments and encouragement as he struggled under yet another load of their newly combined possessions.

Something must have happened to Sylvia after her husband died, Roscoe had decided. Everything became important, not just his clothes and shoes and the briefcase he'd carried every day to work, which she kept like a shrine in their bedroom. It might've been understandable, even, to keep all the things like the wedding gifts that had hardly been used, or the magazine clippings she'd kept in a file for a future nursery. The piles of baby clothes, still with tags, that would never get used, the high chair and the early reader books she still collected could be considered part of her particular grief, but Roscoe couldn't understand the aesthetics of such meaningless things as junk mail and bottle caps and empty little plastic boxes of dental floss and even, sickeningly, fingernail clippings. Maybe she'd saved the few that remained in the clipper, thinking they'd been his, and added to them over the years; there'd been a jar of them embedded in one of the petrified piles that made traversing a path from the front door to anywhere inside the apartment as challenging as a garden maze at night.

Roscoe had walked around the room, holding his silver tank of insecticide, the shock wearing very slowly off. He'd tiptoed around the crushed, chaotic heaps, and felt himself gaining an unbearable weight of intimacy.

She never let anyone into her apartment. Nobody but he, Roscoe guessed, knew the shame piled up inside.

"I wonder if you might have misplaced that box, Roscoe." There was a pleading, desperate look in her eyes. She peered up at him, her right eye twitching just slightly, and he knew that the firm tenor in her voice came at some personal cost.

"No, ma'am. I don't believe so," he said. "There'd have been no reason for me to move anything. But if you'd like, I'll be happy to help you look for it."

She looked at him as long as she could bear then dropped her gaze to his bare floor. He could see her looking around the lower paths of his apartment with something that might have been envy. That's how he interpreted it, anyway. He thought of the horn soaking in his bathtub, the most important of the few things he owned. He'd like to get back to it, really; he always felt a little undone when his trumpet was in pieces. What would it be like to feel such attachment to so many things? To old newspapers and rotten food and fingernail clippings?

"No thank you," Sylvia said. "I probably just overlooked it. I'm sure it's right where I left it." She closed the one eye that was twitching as if to make it stop, then she nodded and turned to go. With her hand on Roscoe's doorknob, she turned back and said, "I'm actually very organized, you know. I'm in the process of going through my things, which is why it might look a bit of a jumble. It just takes a while, to do it right."

"Yes, ma'am," Roscoe said. He dropped his gaze. "I understand."

"I was away for a few days, you see, visiting my grandmother. She fell and broke her leg. They've moved her into a special care facility."

"I'm sorry to hear that, Mrs. Freeman."

She took a sharp breath through her nose, which bent toward her left cheek in a way that had once seemed charming, back when she had a proclivity toward smiling. "I only say that to let you know that if I'd been home, if I'd known in advance that you were planning on fumigating my apartment, I'd have gotten it organized ahead of time."

A moment passed. "I apologize for not letting you know sooner," Roscoe said, and met her eyes briefly. Immediately, hers began to twitch again.

"Just so you know," she said, opening the door, "I prefer to keep things tidy. I just pulled some things out to go through them before I went to visit my grandmother, but I'm sorting through everything now and it's coming along fine. Just fine." She nodded again, as though to confirm some unspoken agreement, and then she was gone.

Images of Sylvia's detritus began invading his dreams like the roaches that had invaded the tenth floor. No sooner would he fall into sleep than he would begin to watch the Sylvia in his dream add to her trash menagerie: pill bottles and bottle caps, newspaper circulars and half-cut sewing patterns, torn pantyhose and used Chinese take-out containers. She moved in his sleep in a kind of slow-motion rush, her sunken eyes glancing wildly around her hoard. It was as though she were possessed by the instinctive ambition of a colony of ants at the onset of autumn, gathering her flotsam and jetsam imbued with some private value; meanwhile the piles in his mind coarsened and petrified and became even more vulgar.

The part of his subconscious that dealt with magical thinking watched the Sylvia of his slumber with some combination of detached observation and disgust. But the analytical part — the part to which he was bound and true — watched with his hands mostly shielding his mind's eye, and it was that part of him that would eventually, nightly, step in beside her and assume the position of one in a bucket brigade. Sylvia would throw something onto a heap and Roscoe would pick it up as soon as her back was turned and drop it into a deep, black garbage bag. In the mornings, when he remembered these dreams over his cups of oolong tea, he thought it was interesting that his dreaming self wore gloves.

This went on for months, this sensate dreaming. And as he grew bolder in his sleep, he even spoke to the Sylvia of his slumber: *Is this how you know the world?* But to his disappointment, she never took up her part of the conversation. Her silence he took as permission, and so he stepped closer to her assembly-line process of turn-gather-toss-turn-gather-toss, going so far (eventually) as to stand immediately beside her with his black plastic bag held open like a maw such that over time, her process was to turn and gather and then toss her leavings not onto a pile but into the bag directly.

Roscoe was pleased. Even if it were only within the pliant confines of his dreams, he began to feel better about the Sylvia of his slumber and even, by extension, the real Sylvia whose treasure was still rendering his monthly fumigations impotent.

The dreams were so real, so tangible, that Roscoe began to blend his daytime thinking into them. He would peer into the oddments of his teacup, searching for meaning. *Stop,* he'd tell himself silently. *Just stop.* But the tea dregs would tell him, *go on, go on.* He swirled the contents of the cup three times clockwise, the way a distant and peculiar aunt had once taught him, making sure the leaves moved toward the rim. He turned the cup upside down on the saucer to let the last few drops run out and then righted it again with the handle toward him so he could interpret the symbols. He'd been told that reading the leaves was like identifying cloud shapes; for each person the same clump or strain could be many different things, and depended largely on one's frame of mind at the time of the reading. So it wasn't unusual that the images he saw clinging to the inside of his cup were things like nails, musical notes, ants, boxes, hammers, brushes, keys. But whenever he thought of Sylvia, the same image always appeared near the top of the rim: a handsaw. According to the book he had on the subject, a handsaw meant something needed to be removed.

The first time he went, fully awake, into her apartment with an empty garbage bag, he could hardly catch his breath. Not from the smell, though it was noxious, but from the chemical rush of fear. He'd been oiling the elevator gate in the lobby when she'd come down dressed for something — a shopping excursion perhaps — and when she passed him, she lifted her chin and looked up at him with her wide, deep-set eyes just long enough for him to interpret her glance as a plea, as permission. As a handsaw on the rim of a teacup. He watched her leave the building and even hurried to poke his head out of the door she'd passed, having just then decided what he was going to do and already feeling the heady force of his heart thrumming wild in his chest. He watched her walk down the sidewalk, hunched against the wind and clutching her handbag in her thin hands. He watched her hail a cab in front of the bakery on the corner, waiting until he saw the driver switch off the light and take off southbound. Once the car was out of sight he went quickly back inside. He'd have run across the lobby, but already he was seeing himself as others surely would: suspicious, guilty even.

He closed the door behind him, muffling the sound by pressing his hand against the lock, and then turned around to face the room. He leaned back against the door a moment, taking slow breaths to slow his pulse. He imagined the neighbor across the hall, the middle-aged university professor, barging in demanding to know his intentions. Of course, he was the super. He had a key. It wasn't breaking and entering; he had a key.

I'm just here because there's something that needs to be removed.

Roscoe looked around at the sunlight streaming in through a sheet-covered bay window, lighting the motes and casting an unexpectedly soft luminescence across the packed floor. It gave him pause and even calmed his nerves, seeing Sylvia's shrine to her inner demons awash in sunglow. He felt a sudden tenderness toward the two Sylvias: she of his slumber and she who'd just gone out for gathering; the only difference between them being that the former was aware of his hauling out bags full of her things and throwing them into the incinerator, and the latter was not.

He decided to remove only what would fit into one bag, maybe less. Though he'd have gladly emptied the entire apartment of its contents and spent days or weeks scrubbing down the walls and floors with bleach-based cleaners, he didn't want to upset her. So he chose a corner that looked the most forgotten and stepped carefully onto it, which brought him a good four feet closer to the ten-foot ceiling. He disturbed as little as he could, even when his foot caught on a stack of glossy phone books at least two years out of date and he slalomed halfway down before coming to a stop against a storage box filled with two sets of hot rollers, one still in its package, a tube of bathtub caulk, a toaster oven, a tangle of phone and electrical cords, and other sundry items that had settled at the bottom. He maneuvered around toward the wall and reached deep into the pile. Before he put it into his bag, he regarded each item, using an unfamiliar scale to measure its worth before deciding if it should go. It took him far longer than he'd imagined it would to fill a thirty-three gallon bag only half-full. He picked up a Better Homes and Gardens cookbook, the pages of which were all stuck together, and saw lying beneath it a small flyer that read, "THE SCISSOR MAN IS COMING." Roscoe took in a sharp breath and looked over his shoulder as though the announcement was about him, as though he'd been exposed, coming as he was to cut out parts of her stash. His heart pounded once again. He grabbed the flyer, which in smaller print announced, "first pair sharpened free and save 1/3 off regular price for all additional pairs," and shoved it into his bag, which he then slung over his shoulder like an accidental Santa Claus whose gift was a theft. Still, the sharp points of taken objects poked through the plastic like accusing fingers against his spine.

All that afternoon he found reasons to loiter in the lobby. When he saw Sylvia coming toward the glass doors and saw the doorman pull one open for her, he felt a light sweat come up around his neck hairs.

"Afternoon, Mrs. Freeman," he said.

"Good afternoon, Roscoe. Is there something the matter with the elevator?" she said.

"No, ma'am," he said, looking at it as if for confirmation. "Why do you ask?"

"Well it's just that you were oiling it when I left this morning, and you're still working on it."

"Oh," he said, flustered. "No, ma'am. I was just ... can I help you with your bags?"

She clutched the four shopping bags she was carrying even closer to herself. "No, thank you. I can manage just fine."

Roscoe barely slept that night. He even kept his trousers on in anticipation of her knock upon his door once she'd discovered his trespass. Finally, when his alarm clock went off at 5:58 AM as it always did and he realized she hadn't come, he started to feel a small relief. But it wasn't until nearly two full days later, when she passed him and nodded a brief greeting, that he actually believed he was safe.

One black bag at a time, he helped her maintain equilibrium of mass. She went out two or three times a week and returned with three or four bags each time. Roscoe no longer had to wait for the cab to pull away; he knew that she would be gone within seven minutes of her leaving the lobby — nine if it was raining — and would be out for an average of three-and-a-quarter hours. He never entered her apartment if someone else was in the hallway, never took more out than she had brought in from her previous excursion, never threw away anything that appeared to have any actual or sentimental value, and was always out within ten or eleven minutes. All the absconded items had long since returned to ash by the time Sylvia came home.

All, except for one.

It was a deviation from his self-imposed regulations, but when he passed through the unusable kitchen he spied a lonesome teacup lying cockeyed on a mound of oxidized batteries of various voltages. It was nothing special really, just sand-colored clay with some darker streaks shot around the circumference. It looked hand-thrown with its lopsided base and uneven handle. But there was a shaft of light coming though a shower curtain tacked above the window that illuminated it there on the pile, like some kind of irony, and Roscoe tilted his head at it the way a dog does when spoken to in some human language. Against his better judgment, for he never touched anything on top, he picked it up and turned it over. Someone — the potter — had carved his or her initials into the bottom: K.L. There was a misshapen heart beneath.

Roscoe thought of Sylvia and her bags. She never bought anything from retail outlets. He knew, because he'd rifled through them. They were found objects, junk from estate sales, other people's cast offs. For all he knew she hurled her fragile body into dumpsters to dig for what only she would consider to be treasure. Where this specific cup had come from was anyone's guess, but Roscoe gave it no particular esteem. It had been made by someone, owned by someone, perhaps even enjoyed by someone. But now it had arrived amid Sylvia's squalor, and with its uneven base and unimpressive markings, it seemed like nothing more than another piece of junk. Yet there was something charming in its being off-kilter, something almost significant in the way the light chose to illuminate it singly amid so many other objects. It looked misfit and bereft of a grateful pair of lips to snug its rim, sipping gently from its contents. It was lost there atop the decaying batteries like an unrequited love, like a missing finger.

Roscoe filled his bag that afternoon and was precisely gone within his self-allotted time. He tossed the thirty-three gallons of nothing down the chute to its cremation, but not the teacup. He held it apart from the bag all the way to the incinerator drawer, intending (mostly) to send it down after. But in the end, he could not. He didn't have the words or the ideas to ascribe its sudden importance, but he felt with his steadily beating heart that he needed to keep it.

He tossed the black bag and hurried down the eleven flights to his own apartment. He immersed the cup into a sinkful of bleach-water, washing it with his calloused hands as gingerly as he would his trumpet. Then he set it upside down to dry on the drain board, and put on his kettle. The thought of his oolong tea drunk from that cup intrigued him so keenly that he grabbed the kettle off the stove even before it began to sing.

Six months later, maybe seven, Sylvia knocked the only other time on his door.

"My grandmother died yesterday," she said. Her eyes didn't twitch, but were red-rimmed and looking a different kind of desperate.

"I'm sorry to hear it, Mrs. Freeman," he said.

"She was a potter. A famous one, actually." Tears threatened. "When I got married she gave me the first thing she'd ever thrown, a mug. And I can't find it." She wept freely then, and Roscoe sucked the breath out of the room in one sharp inhale. He gripped the doorjamb, awaiting the accusation he knew would follow. He felt the shame in advance, recalled the sting of Clifford Brown's drummer catching him with his borrowed trumpet. He closed his eyes, breathing hard, waiting.

"Will you please help me look for it?"

He looked down at her. There was no accusation, just plaintive pleading in her mold-colored eyes.

"Yes, ma'am," he said, and he did. Together they looked through all 1,450 square feet of her living space — more if you considered the surface area of the topography within. At any point he could have stopped her from digging in her own filth. He could have admitted his guilt, brought her the teacup and accepted whatever punishment she felt necessary to mitigate. But he didn't. He picked alongside her, listening to her few lamentations and her repeated excuses for the unfinished sorting, until finally, a half a day later, she gave up.

The next time she left the building, Roscoe stole into her apartment not to remove any of her objects, but to return one. He'd washed the cup and dried it with a soft, clean rag. He knew exactly where he would bury it: one layer from the top of the pile beside her bathroom sink. The one with the half-used cans of Aqua Net and the partly drunk bottle of Schapiro's Kosher Cherry Wine, the empty containers of pain relievers and the tangled knot of pantyhose. He could only hope that she would find it there, thinking she'd mislaid it.

The heavy burden of shame he carried with him for the six years following that day he worked alongside her was something altogether unique. He didn't love her or even particularly like her, but he had continued his stealthy work in her tenth-floor apartment up until that very afternoon, like a penance. But it was more than that. Roscoe felt a kinship with Sylvia; he recognized the loneliness that came off her like a stench. So he did the only thing he could to keep her from drowning in an ever-rising tide of junk, postponing her entombment one bag at a time.

After that day, they never spoke again. They dipped their chins like Geishas if they passed one another in the lobby, in the halls. If she ever suspected him his trespasses, she had the grace never to expose him.

But he knew she'd found the cup; it took her several weeks, but during one of her junkets he saw it atop a stack of circulars. It pleased him that the sediment of coffee inside it hadn't been there long enough to mold.

9

Of the living tenants, Annie Johnson was the one Roscoe would miss the most.

She was going on four years old, with a headful of white-blonde curls and a pair of inquisitive eyes the color of a sun-sky day. Her mother, Olivia, strode her up and down Bellefontaine Avenue in a smart contraption that Roscoe learned was called a "jogger." Annie carried along for the ride a variety of companions — stuffed dogs and bears, bags of popcorn, an unplugged nightlight shaped like a moon — most of which she tossed onto the pavement at some point along her mother's route, shouting in a deepened voice, "Hardee-har-har."

Even through the deafening swoosh of air he could hear her little chuckle that always made him think of Groucho Marx. He had given her a pair of plastic glasses with the fuzzy eyebrows and moustache attached, and for a long time she wore them whenever she went out in the jogger. Her mother didn't seem to mind. In fact, she might have even encouraged it.

How Roscoe would always think of Olivia, when he did, was of her spilling into the lobby at four o'clock one afternoon, dragging a draught of snow-chilled air behind her. She was wild-eyed and stumbling, and when she ran up to Roscoe, who was working on a shorted light fixture near the staircase, and hid herself behind him, he thought she was either drunk or high.

"You've got to help me," she said, glancing at him only briefly before fixing her stare on the glass doors of the front entrance. "Please." She didn't seem drunk or high. She seemed scared. Really scared.

"What's going on here?" he said, turning toward the doors to see. There was the steady flow of pedestrian traffic, heavy in spite of the weather. He watched the parade of people hunched inside their coats, noticed nothing extraordinary. He turned back to Olivia. "What's happened, miss? Somebody hurt you?"

She gripped his arm with a fierceness that surprised him. "Can you come upstairs with me? Annie's there. The babysitter. Or no, you stay here. Don't let anyone follow me." She shook her head and peered around his shoulder at the door. "No, you don't know what he looks like. You'll have to come with me."

"Miss Olivia, I don't know what's going on here. Why don't you let me call the police? If someone's after you ..."

"No!" she said through gritted teeth. Her green-flecked eyes flared and she dropped his arm. "Do not call the police. You hear me? No police." She looked at him with such intensity he felt his rational mind recede. "Now come with me. Please." Once she seemed certain that he would follow, she turned and sprinted up the stairs. Roscoe watched her for a moment, measuring his uncertainty, then put his voltmeter into his tool belt and started after her.

Nine flights seemed like nothing to a long-legged thirty-something who jogged every afternoon, but Roscoe was panting by the seventh floor.

"Come on," she hissed, looking down at him through the cast-iron stairs. "Please!"

He took a deep gulp of air and continued. She pressed herself against the railing until he caught up with her, and then led him at an only slightly slower pace to the floor of her apartment. But just before stepping out onto the catwalk, she flung her arm in front of him the way a parent holds a child in a braking car.

"The elevator!" she whispered, and dropped down into a crouching position. Her scrubs showed beneath the hem of her puffy coat. "What if he came in and took the elevator?"

"We'd have heard the gate close or the motor running," Roscoe said, shaking his head, thinking of all the possible permutations of sounds in the building. He knew them better than anyone. "Nobody's on the elevator right now." Then he looked at her. "Are you going to tell me what you're running from?"

Olivia peered out into the hall, first left, then right. "We've got to make sure Annie's all right," she said, and came out of her crouch like a sprinter off the line but then restrained herself to a more conventional pace until they reached the door.

Upon seeing Olivia, the gray-haired babysitter said hello in a language Roscoe thought could be

Russian or Croatian or perhaps something else entirely, and began collecting her things. Annie looked up from her spot by the bay window where she was playing with a set of plastic Army men and said, in a very convincing British accent, "Nothing but beggars and scoundrels, all of them," then returned her attention to the hooked-rug battlefield.

Roscoe could tell that Olivia was struggling to appear calm, but as soon as the babysitter gave her report or whatever it was in her Baltic language and shuffled out the door, Olivia secured the three separate locks, grabbed him by the arm, and pulled him into the kitchen, out of Annie's earshot. She motioned for him to sit down at the small bistro table, which he did reluctantly, while she gathered her auburn hair into a knot and secured it by several quick twists of an elastic band she'd taken off her wrist.

"Roscoe. It's Roscoe, right?" He nodded, and she took a deep breath. "Roscoe, have you noticed anyone hanging around the building recently?"

Roscoe sat rigid against the chair back and placed his hands in his lap as though they were manacled.

"I'm confused about what's going on here, Miss

Olivia."

"It's a simple question." She leaned forward and put her forearms on the table. That scared look was suddenly gone from her face, replaced by a façade as blank and cool as an empty, snow-covered street. He watched the transformation, saying nothing, until finally she closed her eyes and buried her face in her hands. "I'm sorry," she said. "That came out wrong."

"What am I doing here?" he said.

She looked up at him. "You seem like a nice man. You always say hello to Annie and me." She looked back down and shook her head. "Can you please tell me ... can you think back over the last couple, few days ... has there been anyone hanging around the building? Anybody asking about me?"

From the hollow of the other room came a salvo of shouts: "BANG! BANG! BANG!" Olivia leapt up from the table so quickly that the gasping sound of sucked-in air seemed to come afterward. Roscoe turned and watched her run toward the living room.

"Annie!" she screamed.

"They're retreating!" Annie shouted in return. "Where are my reinforcements?"

Olivia checked the door, then went to the window near Annie and lifted the edge of the sheer to look down onto the street below. But the sky was already dark, the streetlamps lighting the falling snow like shooting stars. If there was anyone out there, she couldn't tell.

"Annie, baby, why don't you move the Army over the ramparts to the other side of the room? Get away from the window. There's a draught." Olivia closed the curtains slowly, but stayed close to the glass. Nobody would've noticed the curtains closing at all, Roscoe thought, not through the snow. He would know. He'd been on the outside looking up at plenty of windows in his lifetime, in all kinds of weather, at all times of day. He would know.

Roscoe stood up and went to stand beside Olivia. He took a deep but private breath, inhaling the scent of her the way a dog does when it tries to know another dog. She smelled vaguely antiseptic, like Band-Aids and alcohol, but upon another inhale, he could discern the soap-smell and the shampoo. Coconut, maybe? And a deeper layer: teeth unbrushed since early morning, sebaceous glands and the metallic scent of unwashed hands.

He closed his eyes. She moved a step away.

"She likes war movies," Olivia said, crossing the battlefield. "It's not something I encourage." She turned to him and wrapped her arms around herself. He could see that she was shaking. "I need coffee. Do you want any?"

Roscoe shoved his incomplete hand into the pocket behind his tool belt. He scratched the back of his neck with the other. "Sure," he said. Olivia nodded and slipped into the kitchen. Roscoe stood in the wood-paneled living room, wondering if he was meant to follow or remain, and to camouflage his indecision he feigned interest in a flickering sconce.

"Are you with me or against me?"

Roscoe looked down. Annie was wearing a drugstore ninja outfit with a plastic scabbard and her mother's sunglasses. She held a plastic sword aloft.

"I don't deal in absolutes," Roscoe said.

Annie flipped up her sunglasses and narrowed her eyes. Then she burst into a chorus of "hardee-har-har" and grabbed him by the arm in the same determined way her mother had only twenty minutes before. He hadn't been touched by any female, much less two, in many, many years.

He allowed himself to be led into Annie's bedroom, whereupon she bid him sit on a tiny chair at a tiny table. She placed her sword between them.

She ducked her head and whispered, "My name's not really Annie."

"It isn't?" he said.

"No."

"What is it then?"

"I'm not opposed to tell."

"Not opposed, or not supposed?" Roscoe said. He had little experience talking to children.

Annie fingered the blonde curl alongside her cheek. "Do you want to play war?" she said. There was a game of checkers on the table, mid-game. Black was winning. Roscoe moved a piece, and with little hesitation, Annie countered.

"Not particularly," Roscoe said. Then, after a moment, "Do you?"

Annie looked at the table for a moment, then up at him with her steel-trap gaze. "I used to have a daddy, you know. But then my mommy —"

"Annie!" Olivia was in the doorway, a mug in each slender hand, glaring at her daughter. "Roscoe, would you take these into the kitchen?" He looked at Annie and then pressed his knees, which cracked as they unbent, to stand. He took the mugs and Olivia closed the door behind him. He leaned his head close to the jamb, his ear not quite touching the wood, but couldn't make out the words. The admonishing tone of Olivia's whisper was clear, however, as was the hurt in Annie's whimpering reply.

The door was yanked open and Roscoe didn't bother explaining the fact of his still standing there eavesdropping. He handed back both the mugs. "I don't think I care for coffee after all," he said. "I'll just be on my way."

"No," she said. "Don't go." She stepped backward and raised her hands in a *stop* gesture, refusing the returned coffees. Roscoe sighed and put the full mugs down on the hardwood floor, which he himself had stripped and resealed just six months prior, the week before Olivia and Annie had moved in.

"I don't know what you did or who you're running from, Miss Olivia, but I don't want to get mixed up in anything." Then he turned on his long legs and strode toward the door.

"No!" Olivia shrieked, and leapt after him. Her

foot didn't quite clear the coffee hurdles, however; the toe of one shoe caught the lip of one mug and crashed it into the other, shattering both and releasing a small deluge onto the floor. The noise and her mother's yell brought Annie running into the hall in her bare feet and almost immediately, she, too, began to scream.

Olivia spun around, saw Annie standing amid the ceramic shards and ran to her. Without looking back at him she said, with fear and pleading, "Roscoe, don't open that door. I'm begging you."

Roscoe couldn't remember when his parents' marriage began to fall apart. It was like becoming aware of a buckling in the sidewalk. For a long time the path one crosses daily, if not exactly smooth, is at least level. Then out of nowhere two slabs have pushed up against each other with such force that one juts jaggedly away from the other. The process is so slow, this expansion and contraction, this uneven movement toward rupture, that nobody acknowledges it. Not until someone trips on the snag and falls.

He was barely sixteen when he finally noticed. His finger hadn't been gone a year. Clifford

Brown's hand-me-down trumpet lay in its velvet-lined case, unused. It was the first time in a decade that there'd been such an overwhelming silence among them. Perhaps it had been the trumpet that had heralded the fallacious sense of peace. Once the trumpet was silenced, the discord was more easily heard.

A boy will go out on the sidewalk and, if there is a ridge in the concrete, he might trip once — but thereafter he will simply step over it. If his father ignores his mother and then becomes sick and dies, abandoning her twice, the boy will step in to fill the gap. If once he has dreamed of becoming something else, he will shove that dream deep into a hand-me-down tool belt and become what he already knows. And he will tend to the needs and, sometimes, the dreams of others before tending to his own. A missing finger will heal. A missing father will too, but it takes longer.

"Don't open the door!" Olivia repeated, but it wasn't necessary. Roscoe was already in the kitchen wetting paper towels. He knew by the direction of Annie's crying that Olivia had taken her into the bathroom. He offered her the squeezed-out towels, but she shook her head. She was picking out the few embedded shards with tweezers, hushing to Annie as she worked. “Thank you,” she said, glancing up.

Roscoe nodded, and went out into the hall to clean up the mess. He could hear Olivia’s low voice speaking that same unfamiliar language the babysitter had spoken, telling her daughter things that Roscoe couldn’t understand and probably wouldn’t anyway. He heard Annie say, through drying sniffles, “Okay” and “I’m sorry” and “I promise” and “I won’t.”

The hallway was nearly restored to order by the time Olivia emerged from the bathroom carrying Annie. The keys on Roscoe’s belt jingled as he wiped up the last bit of liquid. He picked a final bit of crushed ceramic no bigger than a child’s fingernail out of a tiny crack in one of the floorboards. Nobody else would have noticed it, and it wouldn’t have stabbed any bare feet had it been left there. But Roscoe couldn’t help it; he was particular about that sort of thing. Olivia stepped into the hall and closed Annie’s door softly behind her.

“She’s going to take a rest,” Olivia said. Then, looking down at the cleaned-up floor, she said,

"Thank you for doing that. You didn't need to."

He tilted his head at her. "Not much else I can do." A moment of silence passed between them. He placed the shard of coffee cup into the wad of paper towels and balled them around it, oyster shell around an unlikely pearl.

"I can't tell you why he's after me," she said.

"Who's 'he'?"

"I can't tell you that either."

She looked simultaneously young and old, he thought, not unlike his mother when she was Olivia's age. With her auburn hair pulled off her face and her green-flecked eyes set into their dark sockets, she seemed both exceptionally beautiful and exceptionally tired. If she was also untrustworthy or worse, Roscoe decided, it didn't matter. He'd known worse. And really, he didn't know her at all.

"What would you like for me to do?" he said.

Olivia pressed her fingers against her closed eyes. When she pulled them away, her makeup was vaguely smeared. "I guess there's not much point in asking you to stay here. He'll either come or he won't." She let herself slant against the wall and sighed. "Could you go downstairs, maybe, and have a look around? Just tell me if somebody's there you think shouldn't be?"

"What would you do if there was?"

She shrugged. "Whatever I had to," she said. "I've done it before."

Roscoe nodded, then handed her the wad of used towels. When she closed the door behind him, he could hear the separate clicks of three locks being turned.

He walked the nine flights instead of taking the cage. All the way down, he thought of Olivia: her blended scent of coconut shampoo and panic; the brilliant, exhausted green of her eyes. And he thought of Annie, who was so young and yet already burdened with her mother's secrets. He imagined, fleetingly, gathering a few belongings — his trumpet and a suitcase of clothes — then calling Olivia from the office phone and telling her to do the same. He would hail a cab and the three of them would dive into it and tell the driver to take them anywhere, anywhere at all, as long as it was far away: West Virginia or Quebec or wherever it was where they spoke her mother language.

There was nobody lurking on the stairwell or along any of the catwalks on the floors as he passed. There was nobody unusual in the lobby; just a few tenants passing through or checking their mailboxes. A deliveryman walked in with an armful of boxes, for which Roscoe signed. He would take them up later to the recipient, an elderly man who lived with his daughter and two teacup Chihuahuas on the seventh floor. He stopped in his apartment for his coat and hat and went outside, nodding to the doorman, Juan Carlos, who took his position so seriously that he had faithfully refused familiarity with Roscoe and any other building employee or resident in the decade he'd been working there.

There was nobody suspicious outside either. There was just the currently frozen sidewalk upon which he had tread throughout his entire life in every possible weather, often walking, sometimes running, occasionally tripping where it warped, and where he would soon come to a full and final stop.

As Roscoe remembered that snowy night, he imagined them peeking at him through the window sheers. Olivia mouthing the words, *thank you.* And in front of her, Annie wearing the Groucho Marx glasses he'd given her, chuckling *hardee-har-har* and waving.

8

As Roscoe dropped past the eighth floor window he recalled not a tenant, but a toilet.

For months, maybe even years, the toilet in the eighth floor corner apartment had given the tenants grief. A family of six lived there — parents Billy and Brooke and their four children under the age of seven: Banks, Billie, Bailey and Blake — which seemed to Roscoe to be far too many Bs under a single roof. They'd inherited the apartment from Billy's father, who'd died of colon cancer just a few months after Blake was born, and had moved in straightaway with their bunk beds and fairy wings and action figures and art supplies, their sticky fingerprints and tricycle races and shrieking trounces — and an inevitably stopped-up toilet.

The first time Roscoe had been called up to attend the overflowing mess, he'd been assaulted at the door by a wailing chorus of toddlers and a fetor that might have emanated from the tenth circle of Dante's Inferno.

With the youngest on her hip, Brooke begged forgiveness for the smell and insisted she had no idea why the plumbing had backed up so egregiously. There'd been no wrongdoing on her or the children's parts.

"Sometimes people use too much paper," Roscoe said. "Kids especially."

"Oh no." Brooke shook her head. "I've told them time and again about using the right amount. Isn't that right?" She looked at the other three, who stood dumb by the door. To Roscoe, all of them looked guilty of something.

"Have you tried a plunger?" he said.

Brooke wrinkled her nose and shrugged. "I don't think we have one," she said. "Maybe Billy would know, but he's at work."

Roscoe nodded. He'd been doing this too long to take offense. Brooke stood looking up at him with her vacuous, expectant, cheerleader eyes, assuming he, as the super, would step right in to the nicely tiled bathroom flooded with some child's excreta, fix the problem and clean the aftermath.

"I'll just go down and get mine then," he said.

It was, of course, as he'd diagnosed: enough high-quality, double-ply, plushly quilted toilet paper to wipe all six of their bottoms and then some. "You know, the best paper is usually the worst for your plumbing," Roscoe said. "The no-name brands typically go down easier, and they cost less too."

Brooke shook her bobbed head, which looked too large for her body and reminded Roscoe of a yellow lollipop. "Oh I couldn't switch our toilet paper. We've been using that brand forever. Once you get used to something like that, you know? Maybe we should change out the toilet instead. Isn't there something that flushes better?" She wrinkled her nose again and made a small moue of disgust. "Now that I think about it, it's kind of gross to keep the old one. I mean, I know Bill Sr. was my children's grandfather and everything, but you know..." She leaned in and cocked one eyebrow and whispered, "He had *colon* cancer."

Roscoe pressed his lips together. He had a sudden, overwhelming longing for the solitude of his own apartment, and his trumpet.

"I'll have Billy look into it. Is that something you

could do? Switching out toilets? Or do I need to hire someone?"

"No ma'am, I can do it." Roscoe took a certain pride in the workings of the building. It had been his home, after all, for his entire life. He might not own it, or occupy all the apartments, or use any but one of the toilets, but still it felt like it belonged to him. Or he to it. He wasn't ever sure which. So yes, he would install a new toilet if it came to that.

A week later, the new toilet was delivered. A mid-tier one-piece with a high performance rating and a 1.6 gallon-per-flush capacity. Roscoe rolled his dolly out to the sidewalk and talked with the deliveryman, who agreed to help him unpack it and then dispose of the packaging. Once they got it settled onto the dolly, the deliveryman handed Roscoe a clipboard. Roscoe leaned across the ceramic bowl to take it just as a strong wind blew in off the fetch length of Lake Michigan and caused him to nearly lose his balance. He grabbed the toilet to steady it, and once the wind had abated he smoothed his thinning hair and patted his breast pocket for a pen.

He was always losing pens. It grated at him, this particular failure. His otherwise fastidious attention to detail could never compensate for that part of his mind that couldn't ever remember where he'd last left a pen. As a result, he bought dozens of them at a time, always the same inexpensive, retractable ballpoints. His preference for the one kind wasn't the same as insisting on a particular brand of toilet paper; it was simply that he could more easily pretend that he didn't lose them if there was always an identical replacement lying around. He usually kept at least two on his person at all times, one in his pocket and one in his tool belt. But the day the toilet arrived, he couldn't find either. For all he knew, his had blown out of his breast pocket on that sudden tide of wind and was being carried down the street. So common was the act of patting at an empty pocket that it didn't even register as a loss. It would never have occurred to him to look down to see if it had fallen somewhere close by. In a bowl, perhaps. He simply asked to borrow the deliveryman's.

The installation went without incident. With three of the four children watching, he turned off the water and drained the tank, removed it from the old bowl, removed the closet bolts from the base, rocked the bowl free of its wax gasket, and set the sticky, filthy mess down on a sheet of plastic. He stuffed a rag into the drain hole to keep the sewage gases from escaping into the room, but evidently not quickly enough, for the children. "Ewwww!" they shrieked, darting away. The eldest drifted back eventually, however, and even offered to help scrape the wax off the mounting flange on the floor.

"All set," Roscoe said to Brooke, who had walked in to the bathroom to check. She nodded, then walked over and gave it an inaugural flush.

"Oh that's nice," she said. "Very quiet and powerful."

"Let's hope," he said.

She turned to the other toilet, which was lying on its side, and wrinkled her nose as though it were a criminal. "Will you be able to get that out of here?"

He looked down at it and then back at her and said, not without just a hint of sarcasm, "I guess we shouldn't just leave it."

"Good!" she said. "It's really disgusting." She forced a shudder and gave him a fatuous smile before turning back to the children. "Come on, you busy bees. Let's get some lunch."

It wasn't a week before he was summoned again.

"I'm really sorry to bother you," Brooke said at the door. Roscoe gave her a weak smile and held his plunger aloft. "It isn't the paper, I swear," she said.

"Of course not," Roscoe said.

But of course, it was. Roscoe sealed the hole with the plunger and gave it a couple of strong pumps, then tugged it off. Wisps of quilted paper drew back into the pool, along with a backwash of unmentionable brown. Eventually, it was sucked down into the private recesses behind the wall and then underground.

"Would you like for me to leave this one here for you?" Roscoe said, indicating the plunger, over which he'd poured some bleach before he'd left it to drip dry over the bowl. "There's an extra in the basement."

"Oh," she said, wrinkling her nose again. "Well, okay." She looked around the bathroom, which was decorated with tubs of rubber toys and colorful kids' shampoo bottles. On the floor was a fuzzy green rug and a stepstool painted with cartoon frogs. "Where should I keep it, you think?"

Roscoe knew that Brooke had a housekeeper; he saw her come and go twice a week, and sometimes more often if she and Billy went out at night. Perhaps Brooke didn't ever clean her own bathroom, but surely she had changed ample diapers. How could anyone who'd wiped the bottoms of four children behave like such a ninny around a toilet?

"I think you should keep it in the linen closet," he said. She didn't respond, but stood there bouncing one of her B babies and looking at him like she needed more explanation. He cleared his throat. "Do you have an extra pot or saucer or plastic container lid, something you can set down to protect the floor? When you use it — you saw how I did it, get a good seal over the hole and push down a few times without breaking that seal then lift it up — just wash it off and then store it away. Hopefully you won't be needing it again, but there it is, just in case."

"Okay," she said, her face tight with unease. "Should I just let it dry there then?"

He closed his eyes, and then forced his lips into a smile. "That wouldn't be a bad idea," he said. "Then set it down on something like I said. All right?" She nodded.

On his way out, he patted the eldest on the head. His own mother had been so capable. *Lord help the children of a ninny,* he thought.

A couple of months passed, maybe three, without his being asked to help with the sanitation on the eighth floor. He did notice, however, that Brooke seemed less friendly toward him whenever she encountered him around the building. He would greet her, as he did all the tenants, with a polite smile and sometimes a brief few words, but as the weeks went by, she seemed to hurry past him without looking in his direction. It was different enough that he was aware of it, but certainly he wasn't bothered. There were a few residents with whom he would keenly miss making eye contact, but Brooke and her swarm of busy bees were not among them.

One bright afternoon, Roscoe had just finished his homemade lunch — tomato soup and a grilled cheese sandwich — and was passing through the lobby when a plumber came in carrying a tool kit in one hand and a three-foot-long closet auger in the other.

Roscoe wiped an invisible crumb off the corner

of his mouth and dusted his hands on the fronts of his pants. "Can I help you?" he said.

The plumber jutted his chin toward the elevator. "I got a call from a lady here got a problem with her toilet. Do I need to check in or something?"

"Nope, nope, just curious," Roscoe said. "I do quite a bit of the plumbing around here is all. Mind me asking which unit it is?"

"Eighth floor. Mrs...." He put down the auger and pulled the clipboard out from under his damp armpit and looked at it. "Mrs...."

"Bagwell." Roscoe nodded. "Nine D."

"That's it," the plumber said.

"Interesting." Roscoe pressed his lips together, scratched his jaw with the backside of his fingertips while the plumber readjusted his clipboard and picked up his auger. He thought briefly of accompanying the guy, just for the satisfaction of seeing Brooke's face when he pulled out a toy car or child's toothbrush or another wad of toilet paper. He wondered if she was smart enough to feel even a little sheepish for paying a hundred-dollar service call fee plus whatever else the plumber was going to charge her when *he* would have done it for nothing. But then again, the way she'd been acting lately, maybe she thought the plumber's fee was somehow cheaper than Roscoe's nothing.

"Let me know what you find, will you?"

"Sure thing," he said.

A short while later the plumber came back. Roscoe had been puttering around the lobby, waiting. "So?" he said.

The plumber shrugged. "Easy money. Got it cleared out with a few turns."

"Was there anything blocking it?"

"Nah, just paper. I told her she probably could've cleared it with a plunger, but she said it'd been happening regularly even though she just had it put in a few months ago. Said she wanted to get it fixed once and for all." He shrugged again. "I checked the flapper, everything else looks good. I told her if it kept happening I'd have to pull the bowl and check from the underside. But I'm sure it's all good now. Told her she ought to keep the kids from using so much paper though."

Roscoe huffed, pushed a small laugh through his nose and nodded. "So did I."

It was the husband, Billy, who showed up at his office door some weeks later with his hands shoved into his trouser pockets and his tie loosened at his throat, which was just beginning to show the slack of age. The initial B was monogrammed onto his shirt pocket in an elegant script. He had thick, blond hair and the rounded features of a college boy, but a specific kind of fatigue had settled around his eyes and mouth: that of a young man waking one day and realizing that he could no longer fit his worldly possessions into the trunk of his beat-up sedan, that he was now the party wholly responsible for a wife and children and a career he didn't particularly care for, that his ambitions had quietly, traitorously succumbed to adulthood.

Roscoe's first thought was to offer him a beer and maybe some unsolicited empathy, but then he realized that Billy had most likely been sent down on a mission that didn't include fraternizing.

"Evening, Mr. Bagwell. What can I do for you?"

Billy winced, as though he weren't expecting Roscoe's deference. He stretched his neck forward out of the constraints of his tie. "Hi Roscoe. I came down to talk to you about something." He shifted his weight.

"Come on in." Roscoe stepped aside, and Billy stepped in and looked around.

"You've been here a while, haven't you?" It came out more as a statement than a question.

"I have indeed."

"My father always appreciated your helping him. I remember him saying that."

"He was a good tenant, a very nice man," Roscoe said. "I'm sorry again for your loss."

Billy nodded, and shoved his fists deeper into his pockets. He looked down at his shoes. Roscoe wondered if he could see himself reflected in the shine. "So I'm here to ask you about the toilet."

The right corner of Roscoe's mouth drew up in a half-smile.

"It keeps getting plugged up." Billy looked up at him, his speech gaining traction. "Ever since the new one was installed — since you installed it — we've been having problems with it."

"I understand," Roscoe said, puffing out his lower lip in sympathy. "I believe there might be an issue with the amount of paper going down, though. Isn't that right?"

"Well, yes, there might be. The kids, you know, they don't understand how much is too much. But we've been trying to teach them, telling them to use three squares only. But even then, it still gets clogged." Billy pulled his hands out of his pockets and crossed his arms. "The missus, you know. She's getting a little fed up."

"Of course," Roscoe said. He knew how to do that. His daddy hadn't left him much — a tool belt, an unwanted life — but he had taught him how to yield to discontent. Roscoe had learned on his own how to maneuver pique back to satisfaction.

"We had a plumber out and he said he fixed it, but it keeps happening, so we can only assume there's something wrong with the toilet or else with the way it was installed. The plumber said he would take it out and check it, but he's going to charge six hundred dollars and that's more than what it cost."

"Not to mention installation." Roscoe smiled.

Billy looked up at him, cocking his head like a blond puppy until understanding arrived, the way thunder sounded seconds after a strike of lightning. "Oh. Well," he said. "Well, that's the thing. The missus feels that since you installed it that perhaps you'd be the one to take it out. There's something wrong with it. I know we have four kids, but I've never heard of anybody having a stopped pot like this. Something's definitely wrong with it.

And six hundred seems a lot to pay to turn it upside down."

"It certainly does," Roscoe said, shoving his hands into his own pockets and rocking back on his unpolished heels. "Tell you what. I'll do it myself. How would that be?"

Billy took in a deep breath like he'd been coming up short, and then blew it out. Discord probably never was so easily resolved at home. "Thank you," he said. "Thanks very much. I really appreciate it."

Roscoe smiled and again withheld the beer he'd have offered. It wasn't his problem, except that the tenants made it so. He'd go tomorrow during a lull and pull the bowl and prove to them all — the busy bees — that as regarded the toilet, there was nothing but overuse to blame.

That was only yesterday, and today, Roscoe was falling past the very toilet he was supposed to have pulled. But he had not. Instead, he'd taken the day off. He'd had something important he needed to attend in the morning, and afterward, he'd taken a walk around the block, stepping expertly over the uneven seams in the sidewalk. He'd eaten a lunch of grilled cheese and tomato soup, cleaned his trumpet with delicate attention, then had gone up to the roof and played "Yesterdays" for the countless droplets of life below. And now he was one of those droplets, merging with the others.

Right then, his mind called up something else.

That day, many months before. The delivery truck and the new toilet. His hand outstretched to take the clipboard over the gaping bowl. The sucking gust of Lake Michigan wind. His wiry hair, lifted; the dolly, unsteady; the pen in his breast pocket — twin to many — falling, falling. *Clink.*

The wind stealing away the sound that would have told him the pen had lodged into the toilet trap, out of sight. Had he noticed, he'd have retrieved it then. And likely, no matter the amount of paper the B children tried to flush, it wouldn't have gotten stuck. And Brooke wouldn't have had to dirty her hands with the plunger. And the plumber, whose auger went right past the slender instrument, wouldn't have been called. And Billy wouldn't have been sent down to make his accusation.

And Roscoe might not have thought so poorly of Brooke for these months. Or her children. Or even Billy, with his teenager hair and old-man torpor.

His fall wasn't slow enough to stop, however, so he couldn't quite reach out and knock on the glass to say, *It was my fault. It was a pen. I dropped a pen.* He had time to realize it, but no time to make amends. Someone else would have to pull the toilet — that plumber, no doubt. He'd charge them six hundred dollars to do it, and he'd find the pen stuck in the trap. If they were so inclined, if they were smart enough to do so, they might even match the pen to Roscoe's countless others and they would know it was his fault, as they assumed it was. *I'm sorry,* he tried to say aloud into the shatter of memories, into the slow rush of wind.

He thought of Brooke and her monogrammed children, flushing their waste into the void. *Maybe you're not such a ninny after all.*

7

Deliveries had come regularly for the elderly man on the seventh floor, the one with the daughter and the Chihuahuas, once a month at least. The boxes were not particularly large, but they were often heavy and they always arrived by way of an international courier from Havana, Cuba.

As he approached Joaquin Rojas's window, Roscoe closed his eyes. In his elastic imagination he could hear the orotund voice, buried now, reading aloud from *Anna Karenina*. "All happy families are alike; each unhappy family is unhappy in its own way." He could smell the moss-burn scent of the Cohiba cigars, Castro's favorite. He saw the dogs lying rapt at the stumps of Joaquin's legs and the bulging bookshelves behind the couch that contained a dictator's stolen cache.

Many years ago, long before he had become a father to Beatriz — the daughter who, decades later, beckoned him from Cuba to Chicago — Joaquin had been a poet. While the world around him grappled with uprisings and urban violence and economic despair, Joaquin withdrew to the sugarcane fields and that neutral, oblique space where he could slip into the language of youth and articulate all his passions and humors and impressions onto the back pages of his school notebooks. He wrote about the daughter of the city's best tailor, who had captured his heart from across their classroom simply by adjusting the strap of her sundress. He wrote about the Caribbean edge of his knowledge of the world, and about what might lie beyond it. He wrote about his fear of waves and his admiration of clouds and his desire for love. Around the time he was ready to enter University, after several years and six notebooks and two insignificant and one important sexual encounter, he ran out of words.

But then he learned to borrow the words of others. (It would be later — much later — before he learned how to steal them.) One might think a lapsed poet would bear some bitterness toward those whose access to words was still intact, but Joaquin did not. In fact, once he reconciled himself with his disentanglement from verse, he began to truly enjoy reading. He started with Latin writers of the day: Gabriela Mistral, who won the Nobel Prize in Literature in 1945; Alejo Carpentier, a fellow Cubano; Miguel Ángel Asturias, whose novel *Men of Maize* informed him of the threat and delight of modernity. Then he moved on to the world beyond his island border, to the real and imagined lives created by Emile Zola, Miguel de Cervantes, Charles Dickens, Peter Kropotkin (who thrilled and frightened him), Oscar Wilde, Mark Twain. He became enchanted by notables from the Harlem Renaissance, whose skin color reflected his own; Langston Hughes and Zora Neale Hurston were his favorites. And of course there were newspapers and magazines and advertisements and shampoo bottles. Words — those strung magically together by better poets, important authors, even employees of Johnson & Johnson, whose products were still imported into Cuba at that time — became Joaquin's most significant treasures. He would have liked to say possessions, but by then he had been well steeped in the Marxist ideals of Communism, and so he knew he could lay no such claim.

In 1951, Joaquin graduated from the Faculty of Arts and Letters from the University of Havana. He was twenty-one, and he was in love. Ana Albertina Delgado Borrero, the daughter of a prominent cigar factory owner, had claimed him over a heady lunch of *mixto* and orange soda, and had promised him — with her soft hand cupping his acne-scarred face — a life and children and a particular job at her father's factory.

Ana told her father, Ulises, who wanted no such penniless nobody for his only daughter, "But he is a poet! An educated man with a beautiful soul who understands the heart of the working class, Papa. The very people who work for you. He would be an asset."

In the end, it was up to the employees to choose the person for the position Ana had in mind. So she prevailed upon those she knew, and brought Joaquin to the factory for an audition. Not to become a cigar roller, no; Joaquin was to become their entertainment. He won them over with a dramatic reading from his favorite novel, *Don Quixote*. He read an episode from chapter eight in which Don Quixote plans to fight against a farm of windmills that he believes to be giants. *'Those you see over there,' replied his master, 'with their long arms. Some of them have arms well nigh two leagues in length.'* Joaquin emphasized the absurdity by swinging his free arm around in an arc. Throughout the reading, he applied different voices to Don Quixote and Sancho Panza, Quixote's faithful and illiterate squire, using very convincing Castillian accents. When he finished, the rollers approved him unanimously by banging their *chavetas* — the curved knives they used to trim the tobacco leaves — against their rolling boards, and he was thusly hired to be *El Lector*, the reader, the one who sat upon an elevated chair amid the quiet drone of the rollers as they worked the tobacco, with his suit and books and sonorous elocution.

To Joaquin, the arrangement was perfect. Every day, the workers arrived amid the humidity in starched white shirts and hats, which they hung on pegs alongside their numbered seats. Pews, they called them, for they had to pray to God for strength to get through the day, which was long and tedious except for the respite they received while Joaquin read aloud. He was always the favorite among the workers for the intensity of his voice, the complexity of his intonation, his interpretation of the news and international politics, his sympathy with the proletariat — but mostly for the style and drama with which he enacted their chosen works of fiction.

La lectura was a position he would hold for the next thirty-two years, and an identity that he would retain through and beyond a decade of unjust incarceration and an unwilling exile from a country that he loved even more, he would later admit, than he had loved his wife and child.

Joaquin had still had his legs when he'd moved into Roscoe's building some eighteen years before to live with his only and estranged daughter, Beatriz. He'd also had had a barreled torso, a pate of white hair, and a communicable smile that Roscoe, who was rarely affected by anyone, had found irresistible — even more so when he learned, gradually, the series of events that would have turned anyone else bitter beyond salvation. Perhaps it was this trait of Joaquin's that endeared him to Roscoe more than any other, because it was something that Roscoe had never developed for himself.

Roscoe, dropping quickly now, felt as though he were landing in a web of memory that might somehow slow or even stop his fall, so dense was the weave of their friendship. Like a brotherhood. Like a conspiracy.

The first package from Cuba had arrived addressed to *Señor Joaquin Rojas, El Lector* sometime around 2005. Roscoe had carried it up to the seventh floor along with a lunch of grilled cheese and orange sodas, plus some biscuits for the dogs. By this time, it had become their custom to share lunch two or even three days each week while Beatriz was at work. Roscoe could still see the look on Joaquin's face when he'd handed over that first box.

"What's it say?" Roscoe asked, as Joaquin unfolded and read the cream-colored stationery.

"Dice, 'Para el fuerzo de grito.'"

"My Spanish still isn't good enough to know what that means," Roscoe said.

Joaquin narrowed the white caterpillars above his eyes, even as a smile played at the corners of his mouth.

"For the strength of voice."

"Who's it from?" Roscoe took a bite of sandwich. The dogs, still just puppies then, looked up with great expectation.

Joaquin turned the card over then looked again at the front of the package. "I don't know," he said. "There's nothing else but this." He pulled out a copy of *Marianela,* by Benito Pérez Galdós, and leafed through it with his thumb. After a moment, he said in his robust, clear voice, "Do you know this book, Roscoe?"

Roscoe shook his head.

Joaquin took a deep breath, as though to fill the bellows. "It is the story of a blind boy, Pablo, who is enchanted by a young orphan girl named Marianela. She is very ugly, but since he cannot see her, he falls in love with her anyway. She tells him that she is not beautiful, but he thinks she is, because of the strength of her voice." Even while summarizing, his voice carried the practiced modulation of a performer. The caterpillars went up and he nodded his head, perhaps at some distant memory. Then he looked inside the box again for anything else that might identify the sender. Finding nothing, he shrugged. "In the end," he said, "with Marianela's help, Pablo regains his sight. But upon seeing her, he turns and proposes marriage to her cousin Florentina." He shrugged again and made a breathy tsk-tsk sound. "It's the way it goes sometimes, no?"

Roscoe had only a vague idea. He had never read *Marianela*. He had only been in love with one woman, but it was mostly from afar, and it had lasted all his life. And that was something about which he didn't care to speak.

"I used to read this book *en la galera*." Joaquin still spoke a pidgin of Spanish and English. "It was always quiet when I read *Marianela*," he said. "The workers were very affected by that story. But I don't know who would send this to me now. I don't have many friends left in Cuba."

Yet the books had arrived in that way, by ones or twos, every few months ever since. Each time the DHL courier arrived, Roscoe would sign for the package and hold it until lunchtime, at which point he would prepare a simple meal for them to share, his spirits buoyed by anticipation. Then he would take the lunch and the package to the seventh floor, and after they ate — quickly on delivery days — Joaquin would slowly unwrap the packaging and hold up whatever book was inside.

Always, Joaquin searched each page for some clue as to the identity of the sender or the reason behind it. Only once was there a letter tucked into the pages of a book but that was much, much later, after the diabetes had claimed much of his strength and both legs below the knee. And until that letter finally arrived toward the end of Joaquin's life, they were forced to simply wonder.

Joaquin would clear his throat and take a sip of honeyed tea, open the book, and begin to read aloud to Roscoe the way he had to the cigar rollers all those years in the *tabaquería*. Aside from playing the trumpet in the quiet of his basement apartment, listening to Joaquin's inflected reading was the closest thing to peace Roscoe had ever known.

"Why did you leave Cuba?"

"That, my friend, is a long story."

"I've been asking for a long time."

"Indeed you have."

"How can you expect a man who's warm to understand a man who's cold?" This was from *One Day in the Life of Ivan Denisovich*, one of the books that had arrived by courier.

Joaquin looked up at Roscoe. "Coming from Cuba, I could never know such cold as I have since coming to Chicago," he said. "But it was nothing compared to knowing the emptiness of my daughter's heart."

Roscoe nodded, knowing nothing of either the warmth of an island or the love of a child. Their friendship hinged on something apart from that.

"Tell me why you left," Roscoe said, one more of countless times. Finally, after they'd been sharing lunches in the seventh floor apartment for some fifteen or sixteen years and his daughter Beatriz was approaching the time when her father's absence from her childhood had mostly been forgiven for his presence in her middle age, Joaquin lit one of his Cohiba cigars and agreed.

Joaquin was a fat child with drooping socks and a thick chin back when he was a student at La Salle boarding school in Santiago, on the plantar coast of the island. The other boys mocked his unathletic gait and his tendency to bend over his verse-filled notebooks. There was a day when an older boy named Marco, driven maybe by a hormonal surge or some misplaced anger, had passed by Joaquin on the green and kicked his notebook out of his hands like a soccer ball.

"¿Qué es eso?" said another boy who had been playing basketball on a court close to Joaquin. His hands flew up with the question. Fidel was his name, which meant "faithful." Marco refused to back down — they were equal in height and academic standing, and Marco was heir to the largest coffee plantation in Cuba, not the illegitimate son of a Spanish peasant and a domestic servant as was Fidel. But Fidel, with his views against the bourgeoisie already strident, threw himself upon Marco until a priest finally ran out onto the lawn to intervene. Caught in the priest's black robes, Fidel tried to kick himself free and as he did, the priest went down in an unwieldy heap. Fidel was expelled immediately and sent to yet another school.

But Joaquin never forgot him.

Several years later, as a lector, Joaquin donned a suit from his father's meager closet. He had no money for books but he had friends, and his friends had books. He borrowed them to read to the rollers, and as he did so, over the months and early years, he absorbed ideas that belonged to minds more plastic than his own. His thoughts began to stretch and sway toward the passions of those other thinkers, and soon he began to slip away again to the sugarcane fields of his imagination.

Ana, his wife, tried to love the space that he left between them. She didn't know that Joaquin had found another woman, and that her name was Liberty.

Sitting on his daughter's sofa with frost filling the windows of the seventh floor, Joaquin sketched with his hands above his head, filling in the details of his history. Roscoe, who had never traveled further than to Rochester when his mother once needed a cardiac specialist, sat with one leg tucked under the other, listening. As Joaquin drew his past with his squat fingers in the smoke-filled air, Roscoe breathed it in and, in his own small way, became enlarged.

It's not a surprise that by the time Castro descended from the mountains to reclaim Cuba from the dictator Batista, Joaquin was in full support of his old protector. When his father-in-law Ulises realized what would happen to his cigar factory and tobacco plantation when the revolution absorbed them, he told Ana, Joaquin's wife of only eight years, "Are you going to stay here and stand in a Soviet bread line with that fool, or are you going to come with me to Florida to make a new start? Huh, Ana? Him or me. Wealth or poverty?" He lowered his head and looked at her above the rims of his glasses. "You have a child now to think about." It took her less time than Joaquin would have imagined to pack up seven-year-old Beatriz and follow her father, who abandoned both his country and his wealth with a tipped-up chin and a handful of tobacco seeds. Joaquin stayed behind, betrothed now to the revolution and to the leader who would later condemn and eventually exile him.

Joaquin scratched the bare head of one of the Chihuahuas. "Would you like to smoke a Cuban?" he said, winking. The lines in his round face were etched deep, like a failed rift where the smile couldn't quite secede from the frown. "There's another one hidden here, next to *A Midsummer Night's Dream*. What do you think of that, huh? Whoever is sending these books knows me well."

Joaquin explained to Roscoe that he outgrew Castro's revolution the way a man falls out of love with a woman: gradually, until the boredom or the outright discontent makes itself known, or with a return to a former love or the development of a subsequent one. In Joaquin's case, it was that he missed the breadth and depth of reading — even more than the 300-peso-per-month stipend. The squashed, government-approved views of the newspaper *Granma* from which he was allowed to read seemed to suffocate him even as he presented them to the rollers in the factory that had once belonged to Ana's family. Now, it belonged to the faithful.

"But by the time I started to miss my family, I was too late," he said, moving his jowls from side to side. He shrugged. "Ana, she married a restaurateur in Tampa. She had three more children by him. Beatriz was my only one." He waved a finger in the air, and pressed his lips together into a severe line.

The first time Joaquin was reported to the authorities by *Los Comités de Defensa de la Revolución* was after he chose to read Orwell's *Animal Farm* to the rollers who were sweating under a particularly humid summer afternoon. He was cited the next day by two young men — boys — who embellished their authority with puffed-out chests and lowered voices. Joaquin was surprised but not particularly threatened. It was several months, however, before his boredom compelled him to choose something else to read that wasn't approved by Castro's government.

The libraries in Havana were well stocked with publications that nobody wanted to read: The Complete Works of Marx and Lenin, The Unabridged Speeches of Fidel Castro. There were no copies of Toqueville's *Democracy in America*, nothing about the Polish human rights activist Lech Wałęsa, or anything by the Russian historian Alexander Solzhnytzin, who exposed the Soviet's forced labor camp system. Nothing by the exiled novelist Guillermo Cabrera Infante, who had fallen out of favor with the Castro regime. The revolution had failed them all.

Years passed. There were no jobs. No food. No freedom. In 1980, the Peruvian embassy opened their doors and a tide of disenfranchised Cubans swelled the building. Joaquin, bored though he was, and poor, and jettisoned, still held something in his heart for the Castro that he believed in, the one who'd beaten off the bullies, who'd tangled with the priest. One couldn't easily eschew a touch from greatness such as that.

"Don't let the flame touch the foot," Joaquin said, bending forward, his eyes set with concern. "Turn it, yes, like this, spinning, until the foot gets an even burn, yes, yes. Now take it, what do you say, inhale, yes? Slow! Slower, *mi amigo*." He laughed, and patted Roscoe on the back. "Finish coughing, then try again. Slow. See? Taste." He patted the air, as though it were a pillow to be fluffed or a kite of smoke to be translated into signals.

There were to be several more minor infractions reported by the CDR. Then, in September of 1983, as a tropical depression prevailed over the island and bent the palm trees to nearly horizontal, three armed men in uniforms marched into the *tabaquería*, pulled Joaquin off his elevated chair, shackled him and marched him out.

He spent no less than ten years, one month, and sixteen days in prison for the crime of reading

Shakespeare's *Taming of the Shrew* to illiterate tobacco rollers.

Roscoe wondered at the ways Joaquin had insulated himself against all that he'd had to for so long. Their lives weren't so different. The accumulated losses — of freedom, of love, of extremities. Yet Joaquin had found some peace before he'd died. It was that peace that had made Roscoe want to append Joaquin to those missing parts of himself, to round the sharp edges of his fragmented life.

Someone had written to Castro on Joaquin's behalf, perhaps once, perhaps many times. And at the end of the summer of 1993 the squat guard at Joaquin's cell, who had become lax over the years, suddenly stood erect and sweating when he slid wide the iron door.

"*Denos un minuto.*" The voice was unmistakable. Anyone would have listened to it for hours. *Give us a minute.*

Joaquin admitted to Roscoe that he had stood mute in the corner then, abandoned by his *fuerzo de grito.* He was once again the fat boy with loose socks, protecting his written verse from the hails and kicks of the bullies.

"I remember you," Castro said, "from La Salle. And later, the marches. We even kept company for a time." There was a long stretch of quiet as they considered one another. "You believed in the Revolution, Joaquin." Castro could deliver an accusation with the slant of a single word. He emphasized "believed" with a breathy whisper and narrowed eyes, and Joaquin — though admonished — could not help his kindred admiration of Castro's speaking abilities. He was a hypnotic orator. If he'd been born with less ambition, he might've been a great *lector*. "I am told that you were persuasive. You occasioned many people to support our cause through your readings." Joaquin blinked, but said nothing. El Lector had again run out of words. "Yet that is evidently no longer the case." Fidel, the faithful, crossed his arms and paced the small length of concrete.

"According to the law, you are meant to die, Joaquin," he said. Then he turned to the small window and tipped his unshaven chin. He took a breath of the sea air and closed his eyes. Then he turned and leveled his severe green stare at

Joaquin. "I will let you live," he said. "But you will need to find a way off this island that you love."

Joaquin dropped his head, and eventually turned away.

"There is a letter!" he said to Roscoe. He held it aloft, then brought it close to his eyes to read first in silence. He erupted into such laughter that he startled the dogs to barking.

"Well?" Roscoe said, smiling. "Tell me what it says."

"I'll translate," Joaquin said when he caught his breath.

"*Dear Sr. Lector. You will not remember me from among the many rollers who listened to you, but I remember you well. The revolution, while it was still good, provided me the opportunity and education to become a nurse, and for many years I have been employed by a mutual acquaintance that we both once thought to be a great leader until he was seduced by his own authority. When I learned what happened to you, I was outraged, but what could I do? My employer is ill, but he is nonetheless still powerful. Then, several years ago, I had occasion to enter his personal library. Imagine my surprise to find it filled not just with books sanctioned by the government, but shelves and shelves of forbidden works — the very ones that the CDR reported you for reading. I hope you have enjoyed filling your own shelves with these books. I have enjoyed emptying his. Respectfully, Robin Hood."*

"These are Castro's?" Roscoe turned to look at Joaquin's bookshelves.

Joaquin looked also. "Apparently so." His laughter had faded to silence, and then his expression turned dark. There were many years yet unaccounted for.

"Bastard!" he said. Then he picked up the book that had arrived in the mail, *The Foresters* by Alfred Lord Tennyson, and threw it across the room as hard as he could. "Bastard," he said again, more quietly, and he glared at the book on the floor as if it were Castro himself.

After a few minutes, Roscoe pushed himself off the couch and walked over to where the book lay splayed. He picked it up and returned to his place across from Joaquin. He thumbed through it with his good hand and then held it out to his friend.

"Will you read to me?"

Joaquin took a breath and exhaled deeply. His barrel chest rose again and fell. Finally, he nodded. He accepted the book and looked at it. Then he filled the bellows of his lungs again, opened it to the beginning, and began to read aloud: "*These roses for my Lady Marian; these lilies to lighten Sir Richard's black room, where he sits and eats his heart for want of money to pay the abbot.*" He read until the gloaming sunlight slanted through the window all the way to the stumps of his legs, until Beatriz came home carrying grocery bags filled with the makings of dinner, until Roscoe's back ached from sitting in rigid stillness, until Joaquin had lost himself completely in the stolen words.

Joaquin died in his sleep one snowy night the winter before Roscoe fell past his window. The packages continued to arrive at their usual intervals, and Roscoe continued to sign for them. The loss of his friend had become one more burden for him to bear; it was especially heavy when the books came.

On those days, he would prepare himself a *mixto* and an orange soda for lunch and sit down with whatever book the mysterious Robin Hood had sent. He considered sending a note back, letting him or her know that Joaquin had died and there was no further cause for revenge, but he never did.

He liked the idea of Castro's library slowly thinning, and the books, when they came, let him remember Joaquin.

Always the sender included a Cohiba, also presumably from Castro's stash — even though Joaquin had heard that Castro claimed to have stopped smoking in the mid-eighties. Roscoe would light the cigar the way Joaquin had taught him but would simply let it burn against the ashtray, smoke rising into the room like incense.

Then after he ate he would open the book to the beginning, take a deep breath, and read aloud in a whisper, as though the room were filled with ghosts.

6

Roscoe could still remember standing in the shadows of the hallway on the sixth floor, overhearing a desperate, pleading demand: "You get that hooker out of my house!"

How awkward it had been with David and Bill. God, they'd made spectacles of themselves by the mailboxes for the first two years of their relationship. Kissing the way they did, grabbing each other like they were picking one another's pockets. There had been some complaints, especially from the older tenants. But what could Roscoe do? It was the twenty-first century then and he was only the superintendent, not some moral authority, not God. He simply turned his gaze away when he saw them walking through the lobby with their arms linked, gazing at each other through expensive sunglasses.

They put their intimacy on display as though it were a feature in a department store window, thinking everyone might want to stop and look. But they were young, Roscoe thought. They were puppies. They didn't yet know any better.

On the other hand, there was something to admire in their flashy lust, the way they bookended each other's glamorous lives. They were always together, always. They even looked alike: average height, better than average build, immaculate posture, handsome features. Both had dark brown hair, cut in similar styles. They carried matching briefcases. Roscoe had observed enough couples in his more than six decades of living among them to know that they were something else in addition to simply lovers. Roscoe couldn't fathom two men in love simply because of his personal preference, but there was a point in time — it was the day that Bill's briefcase had burst its legal contents and David had rushed the floor gathering and sorting the documents without a second's hesitation, smiling at Bill across the kill of paper — after they'd been living on the sixth floor for two years or so, when he felt something like a knife-thrust in that soft part of himself that separated him from his thoughts, somewhere at the base of his neck. He had recognized it only slowly as envy, that sharp, green thing. He hadn't felt it often. Or perhaps simply he hadn't allowed himself to. Anyway, he'd have bet the building that day on David and Bill living happily ever after.

There was a story about Roscoe's great-grandparents on his mother's side that had been passed down from mouth to ear for several generations. Myth had it that his great-grandfather, who'd been an enslaved seaman of the Washington Naval Yard, took his coffee every morning in a unique fashion: after Charles dressed, his wife, Essie, brewed and poured a single cup—black—and met her husband at the kitchen table, whereupon she perched herself on his lap crosswise, and they began the day sipping by turns and talking. They had modest means, but they had at least two cups in the cupboard. There were countless permutations of how they might've begun their mornings, but they chose—for reasons that were never confirmed but always speculated upon—to break their fast with a shared cup of coffee and their bodies close enough to reminisce the night. They'd married when they were nineteen and seventeen; had seven children, eighteen grandchildren, and more greats than they could count. They'd celebrated their sixty-first wedding anniversary just a month before they died two weeks apart in 1958. Later, whenever anyone spoke about Pop and Gran, they would afterward nod or shake their heads and comment on how rare was that kind of love. His parents certainly hadn't had it. And Roscoe, still wanting his own unrequited love, could only stand apart from the story and incline his head in wonder.

Then came the day when David — or was it Bill? — went through the lobby, head down, alone.

Roscoe noticed him as though he were a stranger, an unpaired twin, after he banged closed the elevator grate and walked through the lobby with a different stride, quick and heavy like a caged zoo animal except that he wore a pink sweater over what would have been a custom-tailored shirt and fitted trousers. Roscoe looked up; strangers usually came in rather than stormed out. It was 7:15 AM and snowing. David or Bill wasn't wearing his coat.

Roscoe waited, stunned, for either the coatless David or Bill to return or for the other to rush out after him. Neither happened.

They'd been gone the week before. Cabo San Lucas, they'd told him, looking at each other and flaring their eyes at some private recognition, their faces shiny as new pennies. They were going to celebrate the fifth anniversary of the night they'd met at a mutual friend's party on a docked yacht at the Canal Street Marina. They wanted to commemorate that happy night near the water, but it was February and Chicago was cold. They wanted to be warm, they wanted something exotic. They asked him if he would keep any packages that might arrive while they were gone, which he did.

They were holding hands when they left, pulling their matching leather carry-on suitcases through the lobby of the building. Roscoe had bid them a safe journey, a happy anniversary, and watched as Bill helped the taxi driver load their luggage while David held open the car door. Roscoe looked through the glass at the spot where the taxi had been before it rushed away toward O'Hare, at the cough of exhaust that rose and dissipated into the cold air. He stood there for some time, rubbing that soft spot at the base of his neck and trying not to think of the exotic vacations he had never taken with the woman he had always loved.

If David or Bill came home that day, Roscoe didn't see him. Whenever he left the lobby to attend other parts of the building, or when he was having his lunch, or after he'd retired to his basement apartment for the night to play his trumpet and brush his teeth and go to bed, Roscoe hoped that the missing half had returned to the other. That night, unsleeping in his lonesome bed, he looked up through the dark at the ceiling, listening to the building's familiar groans and whispers. He couldn't quite understand why, but he felt uneasy. He'd taken a strange comfort in the fusion of David and Bill.

He woke several times from foul and lucid dreams. In one, he'd watched a small group of desperate people eat berries off a vine without using their hands, each of them frantic or panicked or crying, while a voiceover explained that they were eating something called sonosincerity beans which would reveal the truth the eaters desired, unless of course they touched the vines, in which case eating the berries would cast them into a state of everlasting doubt. In another, he was awakened unto his own anesthetized body during an operation — the removal of his right arm — which he could not only feel but was forced to talk about as it was happening. In the final one he could recall, his great-grandmother Essie woke one sunny morning and, while Charles was in the bath, brewed a pot of coffee and poured a half cup each into two cups, and when he sat down at the table in his coat and tie, she bid him good morning and served him his half-empty cup and went outside to break her fast beneath the magnolia tree, alone.

It was three, maybe four o'clock, when Roscoe finally conceded the night to his restlessness. He pulled on his day clothes and affixed his endless ring of keys to his belt. He had no plan except to travel up the guillotine elevator to the sixth floor. Beyond that, he didn't know. There was a dull ache in his head, thinking of Essie leaving Charles to take her coffee on her own; thinking of David-or-Bill wandering the snow-covered Chicago streets, coatless and alone.

"You get that hooker out of my house!" David-or-Bill screamed from behind the locked apartment door. "I don't want to see his face! And you! You!"

Roscoe took a step back, as thought he were the

one to whom the "You" had been directed. His forty-nine keys jingled like a bell choir, and he clamped them with his hand. There was an interlude of quiet and Roscoe looked first one way and then the other down the hallway, trying to invent a reason for his being there in case someone on the floor were to open a door —

David and Bill's door flung open and Bill — it was Bill in the pink sweater — stormed into the hallway, hunching over something in his hands: a piece of paper? A postcard? He tore it in half with a succulent rip then stacked and tore again and again, quickly, until the pieces were shrapnel. Then he turned back to the apartment and, with tears in his eyes, thrust forth his middle finger and said, "Go to hell!" The door slammed shut and Bill yanked himself inches away in a flinch. Then he hurled the handful of paper bits at the door and watched them land in a colorful snowfall at the threshold. His hands flew to his face and after a moment, he fled the hall. He hadn't even noticed Roscoe, who had succeeded in becoming invisible.

If anyone happened to be standing at the window of the sixth floor apartment at the moment

Roscoe fell past it that anyone would have been Bill, because in the days and weeks that had followed that middle-night break-up nearly a year before, Bill had insisted that David didn't deserve any of the comforts they'd created together. Not the Roche-Bobois leather sectionals they'd bought each other one year for Hanukkah; not the metal dining room table and ethereal clear acrylic chairs; not the mid-century Chambers model 61C range they'd found and restored; not even the art books. And especially not the cat, whose name was Mr. Fluffy Pants — even though he was partial to David.

David and Bill may have fallen fast into their five-year love, but after that trip to Mexico they fell out of it even faster. The fact of their dissolution pained Roscoe even in that incredibly short, infinitely broad moment as he passed the emptied nest where Bill and the cat now lived alone.

"Mr. Jones, may I speak with you?" Bill had knocked on Roscoe's office door that next day, still wearing the pink sweater from the long day and night before. Roscoe wondered where he'd slept after he'd run down the hall and flung himself into the elevator, or if he'd even slept at all. His eyes were dark-rung and weary, but his hair was expertly combed. He'd found again his stately posture and he held his shoulders back as though unencumbered by loss.

"Of course. Come on in." Roscoe tilted his head and considered him. Bill looked older now that he was adrift. "Can I get you anything? Are you thirsty?"

Bill pressed his lips together and closed his eyes as he shook his head, barely, from side-to-side. "I'm fine," he said. "Except for one thing."

Roscoe looked at him. Which, among the many things that were clearly not fine, could the one thing be?

"I need David to move out."

Roscoe took a half breath in and then exhaled everything his lungs contained, slowly. He moved over and sat down on the couch, aiding himself with a strong lean against the armrest like a grandfather. Like Charles might have done, with his half-cup of coffee. Bill slid into the chair across from him and leaned forward with his elbows on his knees, one hand cupping the unshaven scrabble on his chin. Was that a bit of gray there? Was it true they could appear overnight? His eyes were the color of the deep end of a swimming pool, which Roscoe noticed only because they were also, at that moment, as wet as one.

"You won't believe what he did." Bill ducked his head and began to cry the deep sobs of someone who'd cried himself well past shame, the weeping of a child who'd lost his lovey, the sobs of a puppy if a puppy could cry.

Roscoe went to find him a tissue. He wasn't in the habit of keeping Kleenex since he seldom needed any and didn't particularly care for the tiny motes of paper they gave off, so he unrolled a sheath of toilet paper and took it to Bill, who dabbed his eyes and blew his nose and tucked it, folded, into his trouser pocket.

"It's my fault," Bill said. "Partly anyway. Do you mind?" He looked up, damp and desperate. "I haven't told anyone. I just really need to get this off my chest."

Roscoe shook his head, attempted an encouraging smile, though he wasn't at all sure he wanted to know the private failings of what he'd thought was an un-wreckable love.

Bill buried his face again, looking old and young simultaneously. "God, I'm such an idiot," he said into his palm. Then he scoured his eyes with his fingertips and blinked hard at Roscoe's hand-me-down rug. "Things were good, you know? Really good. I mean, we made this whole life together. So, okay, sure. So, things might have gotten a little stale in the bedroom. But we've been together for five years! That's normal, right?" Bill pleaded with Roscoe with his pool-blue eyes.

Roscoe nodded, not knowing the first thing about normal.

"First part of the trip was awesome. We laid out by the pool, drank, worked out, danced, made love, everything. Then, day four, after we'd had a few margaritas, David got one of his headaches and wanted to go back to the room. He said to me, 'Stay. I'll be fine.' So I did." Bill raked his fingers against his face. After a while, he said, "What was I thinking?

"God! We have friends in Miami —" He looked up at Roscoe in defense of nothing. "Lots of friends who do it. Just to, you know, mix things up. So I had another margarita or two and I thought, we're here, we're celebrating, why not? So I asked this guy who'd been looking at us earlier. His name was Enrique." Bill shook his head.

"Anyway, Enrique came back to the room with me and I introduced him as an anniversary present and David freaked the fuck out. I mean, he went absolutely ape shit." Bill looked at Roscoe with one eyebrow suddenly arched. "Seriously. I've never seen him so mad. He kicked us both out and called me a whore and said he couldn't believe I would do something so crass, especially on our anniversary."

What would Essie have thought if Charles had brought home another woman? Some woman, perhaps, who cleaned houses in Twining, who happened to be pretty or available or both? How fast would Essie have smashed that one cup to the ground, sending shrapnel like colored snowfall to the threshold of their love?

Bill shook his head, looked up again at Roscoe. "How the fuck would you explain, then, why I found them fucking away like dogs in our hotel room the next day?" His pools overflowed then, and he just sat there looking expectantly at Roscoe with tears and snot eroding the face that only a week ago had looked invincibly youthful. As though Roscoe could be any help at all.

"I don't --" Roscoe cleared his suddenly constricted throat. "I don't really know what to say."

Bill sat up. He sniffed and wiped his face — conscious again of his appearance — with his fingertips. He took a deep and labored breath and straightened his back. "I just need you to find him another apartment in the building. I told him I want him to move out, but he said he won't leave Mr. Fluffy Pants. And I'll tell you this: that scamp can fuck all the filthy dogs in Mexico he wants, but he is not going to claim the cat. That cat is mine."

After a moment, Roscoe said, "I'm not a sales agent. I can't just get him another apartment."

"But you know everybody. You know everything. You're the super, for chrissakes. The Super!" Bill flew his arms up and to the sides like a superhero's, like angel's wings. He leaned forward. "People buy and sell their apartments all the time. They come, they go, they die, whatever. Surely you know somebody who's getting ready to list. What about that old man upstairs? He just died. Is his place going on the market? Because that would be perfect: David would be out of my hair, but he could still see Mr. Fluffy Pants. When it's convenient for me, of course. I'm going to change the locks; he won't be able to come and go willy-nilly. Not now."

"The apartment above yours belongs to Sr. Rojas's daughter. She's not leaving." The moment, strange as it already was, soured at the mention of his friend Joaquin.

"Well, it doesn't have to be that close." Bill scratched his head, and his hair stayed ruffled where he touched it. Roscoe had never seen him look so human. "Come to think of it, the farther away the better. I don't need to listen to him parading around with god-knows-who in the middle of the night. Jesus." He shuddered. "Especially if it's Enrique. I should have known it would end badly when he told me his name. He said to me, 'My name is Enrique. Do you know what 'Enrique' means? It means *enriquecido con vitaminas!*' Enriched with vitamins! Can you believe that? Jesus, why didn't I just tell him to go to hell right then and there? Then I wouldn't be here with you, trying to find a different apartment for the love of my life to live in without me." His chin dropped, then his shoulders, then he crumpled again into tears.

Roscoe handed him another wad of toilet paper.

"I can't live with him, but I don't want him to be too far away, you know?"

Yes, Roscoe said silently, thinking of the love of his own life. That he did know.

"Can you please help me? If I can find him an apartment in the building, then at least I'll get to see him. Maybe that's stupid. I don't know. I probably should give him Mr. Fluffy Pants and tell him to move to Michigan. Or Siberia. Because if I ever see that greasy Enrique again, I'll ... I'll come undone." He closed his eyes and took a long, calm breath. Then he opened them and looked at Roscoe. "If you could please find an apartment that is coming up, I'll pay ten percent above asking. They won't even have to list it. I can do the legal work and they won't have to pay an agent. Please, Mr. Jones. I'm begging you."

Roscoe thought again of his dream from the previous night. Of Essie sipping her unshared coffee, looking at something beyond the leaves of the magnolia tree. He was glad he'd awoken before he'd dreamed his great-grandfather's reaction; glad he hadn't had to see the shock on his face, glad he hadn't had to hear him beg. This way Roscoe could imagine instead that Essie had been sleepwalking, or simply not in her right mind. He could imagine that she'd realized her mistake in time and rushed inside to marry their two half-cups back into one. He could breathe relief when Charles came into the kitchen from the bedroom and she took her pedestaled place on his lap and kissed him. He could go on believing that there would be happy ever after, after all.

Roscoe slowly nodded. "I'll see what I can do. There's a man on three who I think is getting transferred somewhere overseas. I'll let him know somebody's interested. Okay?"

"Okay, yes." Bill stood up and smoothed his pants, adjusted his sweater. His hair, however, he forgot to fix, and it stood up awkwardly in parts. Roscoe would swear that there were yet even more grays. "Thank you, Mr. Jones." He swallowed. "Thank you." Then he turned and went for the door.

"Can I ask — where are you going to sleep? Where will you go until David moves out?"

Bill sniffed once, sharp. Then he shrugged. "The only place I want to go," he said. "Home."

Then he closed his eyes and dipped his head in a slight thank-you bow and let himself out the door.

5

"Mr. Jones," Mrs. Delpy said in her radio voice. "Martin's locked himself in his room again."

Roscoe felt goose pimples erupt through his neck skin. He closed his eyes. Martin.

"I'll be up in a minute," he said slowly, already dawdling.

"Bless you," she said. "The front door'll be unlocked."

A half hour later, Roscoe let himself into the Delpy's apartment. He could hear Mrs. Delpy down the hall speaking in her languid, liquid voice to the door. "Mama's making brownies, Martin. Would you like to help me? Come on now, open up so you can stir the batter." She spoke evenly, with warmth and depth, modulating every word. Roscoe tipped his head so his ear would catch her voice. He'd often wished, over the past five years she and Martin had lived in his building, that Mrs. Delpy would come to his room and sit on the foot of his bed and speak sonorous nothings into the dark until he fell asleep. Even if she did nothing more than count, even if she only read names from the phone book, he knew he would slide past the demons into sleep like a child. With a voice like hers, she could be a hypnotist or a meteorologist on national television, or even an actress.

But she was none of those things, and not just because she weighed almost four hundred pounds and had a snaggled front tooth and let her stringy, gray hair grow long and uneven. For all Roscoe knew, Mrs. Delpy might not even know she possessed the voice of an angel or the power of Hypnos. She seemed, in fact, to care about nothing except for two things: her son Martin, and Jesus.

"Martin, my love, please open the door. It's not good for you to be shut away like that, alone."

"God is with me," Martin said, muffled from behind the door.

"What's that?"

"God is with me."

Roscoe stepped into the hall. Mrs. Delpy sank with great effort to her knees. She put a hand against the door and bent her face closer to the jamb.

"God is indeed with you, my darling," she said in her honeyed tone, "But he doesn't want you to be otherwise alone." Roscoe closed his eyes. He almost believed her. "Open the door, sweet baby. Come to mama."

Roscoe floated forward toward her, drawn by the gravity of her elocution. He could hardly feel his feet crossing the length of hallway, but there he was, standing suddenly behind her. He had to close his eyes for the magic to work; he hated to admit it but he needed her voice to become disembodied to enjoy it fully. The contrast between her slovenly exterior and that piezoelectric quiver was stark to the point of distraction.

"Open the door."

Nothing. Then the muffled, shuffling sounds of a chair being dragged, a door closing. Roscoe, who knew the vaguest nuances of the building, could also tell that Martin had opened a window. There were no screens, because Mrs. Delpy didn't abide them. Once a dove had flown into her open living room window and perched on the back of Martin's chair. From then on she'd wanted to give welcome to any messengers from God, and she often kept the windows ajar even in cold weather, even though they were five stories up. Five times twelve equals sixty feet above ground level. A boy — a man — like Martin might not realize the danger of such a thing. He might not know the consequences of a drop, were he to jump, were he to fall. Nobody could survive a splat like that.

"Mr. Jones," she said, turning her head slowly toward him as though she'd known he'd been there all along, "Would you kindly open this door?" She smiled her snaggled smile, and he closed his eyes upon the visage of her before her bloated features ruined his auditory pleasure. He thought of the boy Pablo from *Marianela,* and he pretended himself blind so that he would hear her resonance without seeing her.

He stepped forward and sifted through the forty-nine keys until he found the one that would release Martin from his self-imposed exile. He held it against the lock for a moment before he inserted it, suddenly afraid of what they'd find. Then he turned the key.

"Gently now," said Mrs. Delpy from behind.

He pushed the door open slowly. The room, at a glance, was chaos. The bed was unmade; the floor, littered with clothes and wads of tissues; the overhead and lamp lights bright even though the day was still hours from sunset. An enormous crucifix hung above the bed and on either side of it, portraits of Jesus that Martin had drawn in the style of a graphic novel. There were dozens of pictures on the walls, hundreds even. In the one beside the closet door, Roscoe thought he recognized himself.

"Martin?" Mrs. Delpy called. There was no hint of alarm, no criticism in her voice. She hurried to the closet and closed her eyes for a fraction of a second, then carefully opened the door. She flipped the light but she didn't need to. It wasn't a large closet, and even with it dark she knew he wasn't there. She spun around to Roscoe, her eyes open like portals. One hand flew to the cross she wore at her folded neck and the other pointed to Martin's empty window, which was framed by gossamer curtains shifting on the spring breeze.

Roscoe, suddenly nauseated, went to the sill. He was in no rush to climb onto the chair that Martin had moved in front of it. He was none too eager to see the broken man-child splattered on the sidewalk five stories below. But of course he had to be the one; no mother should see her child like that.

He stepped up and leaned out, readying himself for the nightmare that would end all hopes of decent sleep for a while, or maybe forever. But when he looked, finally, beyond the ledge, there was nothing. Only pedestrians with their briefcases and strollers and dogs, taxis and pavement and the fire hydrant that had been used twice on the building. No shattered body, no blood, no screaming witnesses.

Then to his left a dove cooed, and he turned. This was one of two floors that were girdled by a light-colored limestone ledge that extended eighteen inches beyond the dark brick face of the building. An intermediate cornice, it was called. Roscoe had always thought it was an overly complex name for a ledge, but whenever real estate agents mentioned it to prospective tenants they raised their eyebrows and nodded. Apparently they liked the sound of it. Looking up at it from street level, the effect was a pleasing pin stripe around the fourth and fifth floors. Looking at it from Martin's open window, it was a death trap. Four or five feet to the left, Martin was crouched against the exterior wall, stark naked and cooing to the sky.

"Martin!" Roscoe yelled. Panic, relief, anguish, anger. Martin jumped a little at the sound of his name, and he made a strange shrieking sound with his dove-voice. Then he stood up, a bit too quickly, and flapped his arms to steady himself. He fluttered on the too-narrow ledge, even closer to the sixty feet of dead space that separated him from the sidewalk below. "No, Martin, stop! You'll fall!"

Behind him Mrs. Delpy tried to squeeze alongside him onto the chair to see for herself that her son was alive.

"Is he all right? Move over. Please," she said, shoving him, "I need to see Martin."

"I'm going out. He's too close to the edge." He looked down again at the sidewalk, then again at the impossibly narrow ledge upon which Martin was standing, and he swallowed the coppery taste that coated his mouth like a film. But as he was about to lift his knee to hoist himself out onto the precipice, Mrs. Delpy pulled him back inside by the pant leg.

"He doesn't know you, Mr. Jones. I'll go," she

said in that resonant, convincing tone. Faster than a rolling O was her voice; stronger than a silent E. "Get down off that chair and help me up."

But when Roscoe looked back down at her, he saw what would happen if he let her heave herself through Martin's window: a fleshy zeppelin hurtling to the ground, the floral tent-dress doing nothing to slow her fall, and then what? A naked bird-man-child flapping his skinny arms and flying off his perch after her, cooing into the rush of wind.

"No, Mrs. Delpy. You just call out to him, tell him he'll be fine. I'll get him. Take my cell phone. Call for help," he said, handing it to her. "Just in case."

Before she could grab his pants again, he climbed out the window. Martin, glaring at Roscoe, shrank into a squat and flared his elbows akimbo.

"Martin, my sweet," crooned the radio voice behind the window, "you do what Mr. Jones says. He'll bring you back to mama's nest, my love. Tuck in your wings, now."

Roscoe pressed his back flat against the brick, holding onto the window frame as tightly as he could with the slippery-damp fingers of his imperfect hand, and to give himself strength he closed his eyes for a moment and thought of the tune "Limehouse Blues" by Roy Eldridge and Dizzy Gillespie — the way they traded trumpet solos back and forth, playing high notes toward the end, all the way up to a double high Bb. And with the tempo in his head he opened his eyes, took a breath deep into the recesses of his aging body, and let go of the window frame so he could inch along the ledge above a fatal depth of sky. A gust of wind off Lake Michigan pulled at the hairs on his arms.

"Tuck in your wings, Martin!" she called.

Martin shrieked again and flapped his arms even more vigorously as he moved further away from Roscoe. His eyes, wide and panicked, darted here and there: over his shoulder, at the sky, at the building face, at Roscoe. His skin was pale — too pale, Roscoe thought — and too tightly stretched over his ribs. He did look like a bird — a baby bird without feathers.

"Martin ..." Roscoe said, and stopped. Slowly, slowly, staying as close to the building as he could, he extended his left hand, his good one, to Martin. "Come on with me. Let's go back inside."

Martin flapped harder.

"Martin, my dove, let Mr. Jones help you back

inside. It's cold out there," Mrs. Delpy said. Against the brick window frame, her fingertips were white. "You'll catch your death in this breeze."

One afternoon, shortly after Martin and Mrs. Delpy moved into their apartment on the fifth floor, they walked down to the lobby and introduced themselves to Roscoe. Rather, she introduced them. Martin stood next to her with his feet in a line, one out in front of his body, the other behind, rocking. He was staring at something on the wall behind Roscoe and as he shifted his weight from one foot to the other, he snapped the fingers of his left hand.

"My name is Janet Delpy," she said in her serene, buttery voice, "and this is my son, Martin." She put her hand against the small of his back, and although Martin continued to rock, he slowed down. He didn't take his eyes off the dust motes, but he did incline his ear toward her.

Without meaning to, Roscoe closed his eyes and inclined his ear toward her, too. Her voice was a compass, a beacon. He hadn't slept well the previous night, and the luxury of her voice made him want to sink to the floor and curl under the blanket of any story she would be willing to tell.

"Martin doesn't talk," she said, glancing at Martin and smiling. "But he can draw. He draws beautifully, don't you my love?" She looked back at Roscoe. "He'll draw you, probably tonight. He has a gift for capturing detail."

Martin rocked back and forth, back and forth, gaining something like a quarter inch each time. *Snap. Rock, rock, snap. Rock, rock, snap.* His gaze never met Roscoe's face. How could Martin draw him if he didn't see him? Roscoe turned to see what it was that had captured Martin's attention. There was a reception desk, a lamp, an eggshell white wall behind it and the mote-filled air in between.

Roscoe turned back to Mrs. Delpy. "Nice to meet you," he said. "Both."

Mrs. Delpy smiled and inhaled a deep breath of new air. She looked around at the high-ceilinged foyer. "If you don't mind, Martin likes to spend time in open spaces like this." She looked at Roscoe. "He'd never hurt anyone," she said, turning the volume of her radio voice low. "People don't always know that, though. Maybe you could keep an ear out for scuttlebutt? Let them know he's harmless?"

Roscoe held out his hand and slid an inch closer to Martin. Down below, passersby had started to gather. Pointing, murmuring their concerns, strollers and dogs and lattes in hand. Martin flapped and shivered, goosebumps covering his pathetic heft, his exposed penis retracted against the lake-licked cold.

"Come on, Martin," Roscoe said. Unbelievably, he was getting comfortable on the intermediate cornice, sixty feet above death. He could feel a rhythm to the wind off the lake, and braced himself against it with the brick against his back. He had known this building from the inside since he was a child, and now he was getting to know it from the out. "Give me your hand," he said. Martin demurred.

"The fire department is on its way," Mrs. Delpy cooed from the open window. "Hold on tight." To which of them she was speaking, Roscoe didn't know.

Roscoe looked at Martin. Skinny thing. How old was he, anyway? Twenty-five, at least. Maybe thirty.

Each time Roscoe moved closer, Martin retreated the same number of inches. He didn't want to be captured, that was clear. And there wasn't room enough on the ledge for a scuffle, even if Roscoe were so inclined. There was nothing to do but to keep Martin company and wait.

The wind quieted, and after a minute or so Martin stopped his flapping and let his arms drop to his sides. Turning toward Roscoe, he shifted his feet apart into his customary stance, one in front, one behind, and began rocking. *Rock, rock, snap. Rock, rock, snap.* He was moving in Roscoe's direction, a quarter-inch at a time.

"How is he, Mr. Jones?" Mrs. Delpy called from the window, her voice betraying none of the gravity of the situation. So placidly did she speak, she might have been asking about someone's distant cousin, someone's pet fish.

"He's calmed down. He's rocking toward me."

"Come home, sweet boy," she called. "Gently now."

In the six or seven minutes Roscoe had been standing on the edge of death, he'd accepted the precariousness of their situation. He allowed himself a long look down. Someone with some sense was shooing back the flock of spectators, clearing the space on the sidewalk directly beneath them. Roscoe considered the crowd. Why would anyone want to stand so close to a bloodbath? A small child pointed up at them. Roscoe waved back.

"Why are you out here, Martin?" Roscoe asked, still waving.

Rock, rock, snap. Martin had covered about half a foot of limestone. Far in the distance, Roscoe could hear a siren. He wondered who would reach him first.

"You must have had a reason. People don't just climb out onto ledges five stories up unless they have a reason."

Martin glanced around, agitated again.

"Please, Mr. Jones," Mrs. Delpy said, low, warning. "Let's not."

Roscoe put his hands in his pockets, but he was not quite resigned. He was separated from death by only sixty feet and perhaps only seconds or minutes because of Martin. Didn't he have the right to ask why they were out there? Didn't he deserve to know?

"He can't speak, Mr. Jones. He can't tell you anything. Just leave it. The fire department will be here shortly."

Her voice tranquilized them both. Martin continued to rock, but more slowly. Roscoe looked at the crowd on the street as though they were the ones on stage. Those down below were the performers, not Martin, not him. Then he had an idea.

"Do you sing, Mrs. Delpy?" he said.

"Do I sing?"

"Yes," he said, watching Martin. "Do you sing?"

"Might we talk about that after my son and you are safely inside?"

"I was thinking," Roscoe said, without turning his head. "If you were to sing something, maybe he'd come closer to us." But he had to admit, dangling in the wind, vulnerable to whatever fate would do, that he would like nothing more than to hear Mrs. Delpy sing.

"Well, yes," she said, "I used to. But since ... I haven't ... for a long time."

"How about 'Bye Bye Blackbird'?" he said, quickly. "But slow. Can you do that?"

There was a pause. Roscoe looked at Martin, whose head had cocked at a particular angle. He couldn't talk, but he could hear. He could listen.

Then from the window, slow and deep and unexpectedly sure: "*Pack up all my cares and woes, feeling low, here I go, bye bye blackbird ...*"

Roscoe watched Martin close his eyes.

"Where somebody waits for me, sugar sweet so is she, bye bye blackbird."

The siren wailed nearer, almost an accompanist. Roscoe's nine fingers ached for his trumpet and a B-flat note. A new breeze licked him back against the building. Why had he never thought to ask her to sing before?

"No one seems to love or understand me, and all the hard luck stories they keep handing me. Where somebody shines the light, I'll be coming home tonight, bye bye blackbird."

The crowd below parted and the fire truck pulled alongside the cracked sidewalk and unfurled its articulated boom lift.

No one seems to love or understand me ...

Someone — a firefighter — was speaking at them through a megaphone, but Roscoe couldn't make out what he was saying. He saw the yellow turtle hat, the bunker gear, the basket rising up toward them, defying gravity one foot at a time. He looked at Martin, who'd stopped his rocking and was instead watching a pair of mourning doves who'd flown up and perched on the limestone cornice between them. Mrs. Delpy's messengers from God.

... and all the hard luck stories they keep handing me ...

Roscoe moved toward the doves, toward Martin. The boom lift rose. Mrs. Delpy sang. The crowd watched. Was there a God?

... Where somebody shines the light ...

Martin closed his eyes again, and Roscoe moved closer. The birds swiveled their heads. Who knew what they were thinking, if anything?

... I'll be coming home tonight ...

The firefighter who met them at the edge of eternity was young — too young, Roscoe thought, to be so elevated — but he smiled as he reached out his ungloved hand toward Roscoe.

"No." Roscoe shook his head. "I'm fine." He inclined his head. "Get the boy first."

Gently, the firefighter took hold of Martin's arm and helped him into the basket. He took off his coat and put it around Martin's bird-like shoulders. Once inside, Martin planted his feet in his comfortable way and began rocking once again. *Rock, rock, snap. Rock, rock, snap.* But he was safe now. Roscoe would install burglar bars that very day to ensure that such a flight would never happen again.

The firefighter then extended his hand to Roscoe. Roscoe met it with his own, the defective one, the one with the missing middle finger, and he clasped the young man's capable hand and allowed himself to be led into the basket next to Martin.

... Bye bye blackbird.

"Thank you," Roscoe whispered.

But to whom he was speaking, even he wasn't sure.

4

Herbert Dunne sank into the cushions of a Heywood-Wakefield club chair, the most recent addition to the apartment he was decorating in anticipation of Patty's moving in. With his socks on, he rested his feet against the bay seat and stared out the open window at the orange-pink clouds. A moment ago, he'd been listening to a wonderful version of the tune "Yesterdays" that was floating through the cool October air — probably from somebody else's open window. He wasn't much of a jazz aficionado, but he knew that song because his grandmother, Irene, had starred in a movie from the thirties in which that song was featured. He wished Patty were there to watch the sun set over the lake and listen to that hauntingly lovely song. He'd tried to get her to watch some of Irene's movies, but she hadn't had the patience for them. "I'm sorry. I know she's your grandmother," she'd said. "But they're just so ... stilted."

He sighed, and let his head drop back. His neck was sore and he was fighting a cold. He thought about getting up to pour himself a drink, but his body felt too heavy to move. How nice it would be if Patty were there to rub his shoulders. Just the idea of her hands on his tired muscles made him ache. He closed his eyes and let out a deep breath, lost again in the familiar eddy of longing. He hardly noticed the fleet shadow that eclipsed the setting sun for less than a moment. It might have been a bird, or a cloud, or his own mind playing silly tricks to pass the solitude of his captivity. He didn't know that it was the body of the building superintendent plummeting past his floor-to-ceiling window. Roscoe was gone before Herbert knew it.

Another loss among many.

A tri-tone text notification sounded out of Herbert's pocket. He leaned back to excavate his phone from the tailored Italian wool slacks, flat-front, suggested by Patty. She'd encouraged him at some point along the way — with carefully measured doses of sarcasm that were only slightly jarring — to jettison the comfortable pleated trousers, the inexpensive jeans, the house in the suburbs, the wife. The children.

Not going to be able to sneak out 2nite. So sorry. Hopefully this weekend. He's going out of town. XO

He read it again, and squeezed the phone as though it were a throat. He'd have hurled it out the open window and let it shatter into shrapnel on the sidewalk, but he knew enough even in anger to know he'd regret it. For four years, it had been his only reliable connection to her.

Are you sure? With his finger hovering above the SEND button he read it again, then backspaced until the line was empty. *No worries. Long day. I was going to suggest postponing.* He paused. *I love you. XO*

"Bitch," he said aloud.

"What will it take?" he'd asked her a few months in. "Leave him. I'll leave her. What will it take?"

It was the art opening of one of her many friends at a new gallery in Wicker Park. They were standing side by side in an aggressive square of light, looking at a crumpled piece of paper that was actually sculpted out of cedar.

She shook her head without turning to him. “You know I love you.”

“So leave him,” he said, the crumpled wood suddenly a metaphor for a wasted life. “Don’t you want to be happy?”

“I am happy,” she said. She reached for his hand and squeezed it quickly before letting it drop. She was never reckless in public.

Herbert stood and looked out the window at the silver-scaled glimmer of lake in the distance. Patty was probably going to an event with her husband, Bob. He could just imagine her, dressed in something clingy and current, wearing a pair of those insidious heels that he knew pinched her toes. She’d had her breasts done during their first year together — at Bob’s behest, not his. In fact, he’d begged her not to do it, had tried for weeks to convince her of her own natural beauty, touching her with careful attention whenever he could, which was never enough — two or three times a week at the most. She went through with it anyway, and it was he who drove her to the surgical center and paced in the waiting area until the nurse came out to report that all had gone “magnificently,” then took her home and cared for her while her husband was in New York scouting new commercial real estate opportunities and the nanny was taking care of her two children in their second home, across the lake in Michigan.

She'd been an ungracious patient. Demanding and whiny. He had maneuvered around the home she shared with her family, cooking for her as well as he could, trying to make her comfortable. Everywhere, it seemed Patty and Bob and their children's faces smiled out at him from the silver frames that served to document their lives: their sailing trips to the Bahamas, endless charity galas, the safari they'd gone on right after Herbert and Patty had consummated their attraction. Until recently, those two weeks she'd spent alongside Bob as he hunted zebra and baboons and wildebeest in east Africa were the longest he'd suffered in the past four years.

When the bandages came off, she cried. They were too big, she said. What had she done? He tried to admire them, to reassure her that she was beautiful, to remind her of what the doctor had said about it taking months or even a year for them to seem natural.

Truth was he didn't like them, even after a year had passed. He missed her old breasts, with their faint, silvery stretch marks and soft droop. The pliant nipples that were the only physical reminder that she'd ever been remotely maternal or domestic. The new breasts made her look younger, yes, and with her blonde hair and white smile and Pilates-taut body, he might have found her even more attractive. But the implants stood firm in his path to the center of her heart, which was the X on the grand treasure map he'd written in his imagination.

It wasn't even that he loved her so much as he *needed* her. He needed to win her. He needed to possess and inhabit her. If he did, then, well, he might finally be able to rest in something like contentment. Of course he also loved her — he loved her more than he'd ever loved anyone, more than his wife who'd become a disappointment, his job, his friends, even, possibly, his children, whose attachment to him had slackened more with each passing year.

That she was not willing or able to love him back completely made the treasure hunt that much more frenzied. Outward, he was the deft adult, calm and capable, proportionate in his responses.

Inside, his angst roiled, rattling the cage of his juvenile heart.

It had been three years since they met at the Holocaust gala. He'd been invited by a long-time client. Somehow, he'd caught her wandering green eye.

"You're that architect," she'd said, slurring only slightly.

"No," he'd said, buoyed by a few whiskey sours. "I'm that insurance agent." He'd had the courage to wink, which she'd — unbelievably — found funny. She'd laughed and laughed, coughing into her cocktail napkin, and he'd held her elbow and laughed too, but aware of the pretense as though he were the devil on his own shoulder.

"I'm Herbert."

She looked at him, suddenly sober. "Herbert? Really?"

He wrinkled his nose and lifted his thick Semitic eyebrows at her, toggled an imaginary cigar. She pressed her hand to her mouth and closed her eyes.

"I think I love you," she finally said. "Herbert."

"And I think I love *you*."

She led him by the hand out of the banquet room and into the server's hall, waving genially at anyone who caught her eye as they passed. "Hide it all in public," was the motto she later claimed. A squat woman in black and white passed, carrying several open bottles of wine. Patty reached out and took one from her with a nod and badly-pronounced *gracias*, and giggled. "Come on," she said.

"What about your husband?"

"My husband is a self-obsessed, egomaniacal asshole," she said. "He'd no sooner notice if I were to lay spread-eagle on the banquet table with you between my legs than if I were dancing the Macarena on stage." She handed him the bottle and he took a swig and handed it back to her.

"Why me?" he asked.

She looked at him for a moment, eyes alight: appraising him from the top of his full, dark head of hair, past his grey-mottled beard and his only slightly distended abdomen, down to his solemn loafers. Then she laughed. "Because you seem to see me," she said. She took the bottle from him. "I'm Patty. What's your name again?"

"Thank you, Mr. Jones."

Roscoe had looked over his shoulder at him, drill held high. "No trouble."

"I mean it. I'm sorry I called you up this time of night. But my ... girlfriend, she's going to be moving in, and I want things to look exactly right. You think you can fix that hole?"

"Sure I can."

"I've hung curtains before. Of course."

"Studs can be hard to find."

Herbert coughed into his fist. "Maybe a little higher? She said they should just sweep the floor."

Roscoe patched the gaping, vaginal space that Herbert had drilled into the sheetrock then found the studs that would bear the weight of Patty's drapery.

Herbert slipped away and returned with two bottles of beer. He offered one up to Roscoe, who shook his head.

"Thank you kindly, but I don't drink while I'm working."

"Oh," Herbert said. Then he sat down on the Eames chair that faced the dining room and rested both arms on the armrests. "Well, I do," he said into the sound of the drill, then took a long swig from one and then the other bottle.

Now, as Roscoe was skimming the windows of the building, Herbert pushed himself off the uncomfortable contours of the Heywood-Wakefield chair. He smoothed the flat front of his trousers and looked out at the orange-worsted gloaming and the glimmer of the lake. He went into the bedroom, and from the nightstand, he withdrew a box of hollow-points and the revolver that had belonged to his father.

Maybe he couldn't hang a width of velvet curtains, but he knew how to handle a gun. It was the only thing his father had ever cared to teach him. And he preferred jacketed hollow-point bullets, mostly because that's what his father used but also because he preferred to hit a target at close range. "One of them rounds'll go through the chests of two men before lodging into the heart of a third," his father had told him long ago. "Not the sort of thing you want to unload in your own home, or even on a city street—unless you have specific intentions."

The flat-front pockets were still foreign-feeling, but they were also shallow and convenient. He filled them with extras, though he wouldn't need them. His father had taught him well.

There were only so many celebrity events on any given night. He used his phone — thankfully he hadn't thrown it out the window — to narrow the search. Bob Bullion was to be honored as a Justice for Kids Hero Award recipient at that night's fourteenth annual gala. The blurb on the society blog read:

> *The voice for neglected and abused children, those forgotten and lost. Providing safety via legal support and vigilance, we seek to educate victims, families, front-liners and the community. In a world where kids have no voice, we are often their last hope.*

Herbert cleared the browser cache and then loaded the six rounds. Bob didn't give a shit about abused children. He didn't even care about his own kids. According to Patty, he'd never changed a diaper, attended an open house, helped with homework, or tucked a child into bed. He made two million dollars a year, and he said that bought him the right to hire someone else to do it. He didn't even want Patty dealing in domesticity. Her job was to look good on his arm, to smile white, and to sound reasonably intelligent at parties. The children will be grown and gone soon enough, Bob had said to her — and she'd in turn said to Herbert — so you might as well focus on the things that last.

"What will it take?" he asked her.

She sighed and pulled the sheet up to the underside of her new breasts. They were like ramparts against a romantic landscape. "Build me a castle," she said. "A mid-century modern castle with ten-foot windows and a butler's pantry. In the middle of the city. Purple velvet curtains that sweep the floor and a walk-in closet that holds four hundred pairs of shoes."

"Done," he said, and he patted her gently on the stomach, which she clenched in response. She rolled over so that her back was to him but let him press against her. "I love you," he whispered in her ear. He breathed in the scent of her: milk and honey body lotion, a perfume that smelled of fruit and wood and patchouli. He closed his eyes. He could live off the richness of her odor.

"I love you, too," she said, automatic and rushed. She was asleep within minutes but he lay there alongside her in the dark, awake for hours, barely breathing to keep her from waking. If she woke, she would leave. She'd never, in all their years together, spent an entire night.

There were things he didn't know about her. Whether she flirted with other men, whether she had any other lovers. To whom she told her secrets — which she guarded from him — or whom she considered her second-best friends. What her childhood fears had been, how often and where she masturbated if she did, what made her happiest at the end of a day. He knew her social security number, her mother's maiden name, her date of birth—and those of her husband and children. He'd become their insurance agent after they'd fucked a third time.

He also knew that Bob had a heart condition. High blood pressure. He was on angiotensin-converting enzyme inhibitors, calcium channel blockers, and beta blockers. He carried nitroglycerin tablets in the glove compartment of his Bugatti. No amount of liposuction or Botox or spray tanning could change the immutable fact of his fifty-six years. With a revolver pressed against Bob's lifted temple, Herbert might not even have to pull the trigger.

He looked around the finished apartment, the castle in the middle of the city. Everything was ready. The closet, the pantry, the curtains. In fact, he'd done far more than she'd thought to request. A mid-century brutalist aesthetic throughout. Custom bamboo cabinets. A pseudo-sunken living room. Artwork by Camille Graeser and Francis Berry and Lamar Briggs. It hadn't been easy. There'd been a lot to learn about the world in which she lived. It had cost him everything he'd saved and more. But for reasons he couldn't quite explain, she was worth it.

He tucked the revolver into his waistband and put on his sport coat. He took a breath and smoothed his front. He opened the door, then turned and took a last look at the apartment. The purple velvet curtains framed the sunset in a dramatic sweep. He made a mental note to thank Roscoe next time he saw him for a well done job. Then he smacked the light switch with an open palm and closed the dusk-lit room behind him.

He couldn't wait to bring Patty home, once and for all.

3

He had been falling at a predictable, mathematically accurate velocity, but as he dropped past Janie White's third floor window, Roscoe felt himself begin to slow. He couldn't possibly be, he knew; he wasn't a betting man, but if he had to predict a winner in his current contest with gravity, it wouldn't even be close. But still, as he craned for a glimpse into Janie's apartment, he felt the air catch around him, holding him just a moment longer than he'd come in the past few milliseconds to expect. In that extra gift of time, he wanted more than anything to see Janie standing there in her nurse's uniform, her arm hooked around the waist of someone who loved her, looking out onto the sunset from a shared perspective. He wanted catch her glance as he fell, just long enough to nod his approval. His forgiveness, he hoped, she already knew she had.

The third floor corner apartment was occupied by three tenants: sisters Trudy and Janie White and Trudy's best friend from childhood, a former model and current high school math teacher named Isa Gomez. Trudy was a commercial pilot who flew an international bid out of O'Hare and was gone more often than she was home. Janie was a trauma nurse who worked the graveyard shift at Northwestern Memorial. None of them could afford that apartment alone, so they'd agreed to share it. It was convenient to the airport, the high school and the hospital, and their schedules aligned for minimal overlap. Each could almost pretend she had the place to herself. Well, certainly Trudy and Isa could. For Janie, it wasn't quite so easy.

Janie worked five nights a week from 9 PM until 5 AM. She'd accepted the job because she could earn more than she would by working a day shift. Her plan was to build her savings so that eventually, when she found love, she could choose to stay home and raise a family without feeling guilty. Though according to her mother, she would probably feel guilty anyway. Eventually, Janie came to appreciate the rhythm of the night shift: stretches of relative calm punctuated by adrenaline-spiking emergencies. Like the other nurses and night staff, she became an outlier, living a schedule opposite that of the rest of the world. She got along fine with everyone, and was even respected by the doctors for her skills and work ethic. She might have developed some good friendships, maybe discovered a love interest in one of the hospital employees, but she tended to drift toward the edges of a room. A lifetime of living in her sister Trudy's shadow had made her shy. So she took her breaks alone with a snack and a book. Even she had lost count of how many times she'd sat down with her old copy of Jane Austen's *Persuasion* while helping herself to whatever sweet treats someone had left out in the kitchen.

After two years of living her inverted life, her savings account was more substantial but unfortunately, so was her weight. And whether it was because she lived her life while everyone else was sleeping or because she agreed with her mother that she wasn't terribly pretty or interesting to begin with or because her flesh now strained unappealingly against her scrubs, she was no closer to finding her own Captain Wentworth with whom she could finally begin living happily ever after. And as if that weren't bad enough, it seemed like every morning she had to go home to the leavings of one of Isa's parties.

Isa could not have been more opposite Janie. Stylish and sleek, always moving with a certain grace reminiscent of the old-time screen stars. The Lauren Bacalls and Rita Hayworths, those smoldering, chin-down glances, the head-back laughs. She was the type who'd have made smoking seem glamorous again if she'd chosen that vice, but she was mostly against it, because it would've interfered with her martial arts practice. She spent her math teacher salary on designer clothes bought at discount stores, meals out at hip restaurants, and cheap vodka which she started drinking every day at 5:45 PM, as soon as she got home from the dojang and hung her black belt over her closet door. Janie would emerge from her pre-shift nap about the time Isa was on her second vodka tonic, and as soon as Janie was gone, with hardly any words exchanged, the inevitable bevy of drinkers and friends would begin to arrive.

Of those who kept Isa company, only Trudy and Janie knew the ragged lot she'd been born to. The White family had absorbed her into their home sometime around the end of Trudy and Isa's eighth grade year, when Isa came over with one too many bruises. Her nightmares had kept them all awake that first week, and by the time she was able to sit at the dinner table without crying, they'd already decided she shouldn't go back home.

"Filthy dogs," Janie said under her breath as she carried four half-empty glasses into the kitchen. She didn't want to wake either Isa or the unidentified naked man who was sprawled across Isa's bed. That was how it was. Janie, tired and loaded on adrenaline and coffee and sugar, coming home to the apartment she paid an equal share of rent for but around which she did most of the heavy lifting. There were always half-empty glasses and half-full ashtrays. Dirty dishes on the coffee table and on the floor by the couches. And there was almost always a naked man passed out somewhere. Once, there'd been two. By the time Janie had finished cleaning up the mess, Isa's clock would go off with its shrill alarm and there would be a slow rustle of sheets as someone reached across the bed for the snooze button.

Without a sound, Janie folded the dishcloth and draped it over the empty sink and retreated to her own bedroom with a quiet click of the door before she had to face anyone directly. She lay down on her bed, letting out a heaving sigh as she did so, wincing at the creak of springs beneath her. She rolled to the side, her shoes still on, and picked up her other copy of *Persuasion*, which was tented on her bedside table. The pages were worn thin, dog-eared, with so many passages underlined as to be rendered meaningless. But it was a comfort, a talisman. She thumbed the fore edge in a game of literary roulette, stopping at random within chapter eight. She spread it open and read the first passage her eyes met, aloud into the quiet:

"His cold politeness, his ceremonious grace, were worse than anything."

"Honestly, Janie, I don't know why you don't find something else to read."

Janie slapped the book closed and wrestled herself to a sitting position. Isa leaned against the open doorframe, pushing her long hair off her face.

"I don't know why you don't knock first," Janie

said.

"Whatever." Isa ticked her head back in the vague direction of her own room. "I just wanted you to know that Kevin's still sleeping. I didn't want you to freak out after I left for work."

"Kevin?"

Isa rolled her eyes. "As if you didn't see him. He's the hot one. In my bed." She unbuttoned the oversized, wrinkled dress shirt she was wearing — Kevin's presumably — and let it hang loose. It had the grating effect of making her already perfect body look even more tan and slender inside it. Janie looked away. "He'll be out of here by eight, he has to be at the lab by nine."

"What lab?"

"Who fucking cares what lab?" Isa closed her eyes and pinched the bridge of her nose.

"Why are you such a bitch, Isa?" Janie looked up at her, not moving, no threat or malice in her voice.

Isa took a sharp breath in, then narrowed her eyes and exhaled, slowly. She shifted her weight, brought her hands carefully to her hips inside Kevin's shirt so that her body was on full display. "I don't know Janie. Why are you so fat?"

Janie wanted to look away but she didn't. She

would let her eyes dry and peel before she so much as blinked. She looked directly at Isa until Isa dropped her eyes and then her hands and finally turned away.

"Sorry," Isa said to the floor. "I shouldn't have said that." She waited without looking up, waited as though Janie might forgive her or at least say something, anything to which she might reply with a softer tone, but Janie said nothing and eventually, Isa left. A moment later, Janie heard the shower running.

Janie lay back down on the bed, her book closed upon her chest. *His cold politeness.* She folded her hands across her belly. Pushed down, to test the give. She'd been thin as a child. Never had to worry about her weight. She'd liked reading more than sports or friends even then, but nobody had ever criticized her for it.

The hairdryer blew Isa's long hair straight. The grainy roll of the drawer meant she'd applied her makeup. The faint slam of door meant she'd left for the workday, to teach the bewildered and beguiled their tenth grade math.

Janie picked up her book again, scanned a page without absorbing it then put it down. She thought of Isa in that shirt, perfect, perfectly formed. She thought of herself. *His ceremonious grace.* She remembered the first day she'd met Isa, when she was eleven and Trudy was thirteen. She'd been sitting on the couch, reading. Trudy and Isa had come tumbling in, wet from swim team practice, giggling and shoving, their tan bodies already budding. Janie had looked, then tried not to look. They giggled still, absorbed in the moment of teendom and angst and passion. Janie looked down at herself, her shapeless, pale legs that had never known a sport, and she knew then that she would always be something apart from their world.

After she heard the front door close, she went into the cleaned-up kitchen to make herself a meal.

She resolved, right there and then, again, to lose weight. No more bagels with cream cheese at the start of a shift. No more donuts or cookies or whatever happened to be lying around for the taking during breaks. She was a nurse, after all. She knew what the human body needed and didn't need. And she was a decent cook when she wanted to be. She pulled out a carton of eggs and checked the expiration date. Rummaged through the crisper and found celery, a bell pepper, an onion — the mirepoix her Cajun mother had fed them on growing up. Salt and pepper. She opened the cheese drawer and saw the package of thick-cut bacon and she shut it, fast. *No,* she told herself. *Not until you lose thirty pounds.* That sounded very far away. *Okay, twenty.*

Soon, she'd filled the apartment with the scent of the holy trinity sautéed in olive oil. Just as she was pouring the six whipped egg whites onto the skillet, the mysterious Kevin shuffled into the kitchen.

"Hey," he said.

Janie jumped, and as she spun around, the edge of her free hand glanced against the skillet, not long, not hard, but enough to sear a crescent-shaped burn into the flesh. "Oh!" she said and grabbed herself, twisting her hand over to look at the wound. "Damn it!"

Kevin moved forward and took her hand. "Here," he said, and pulled her to the sink. "Run some cold water over it."

Janie snatched her hand back and looked up at him. He was appallingly beautiful. Longish hair raked back from his face, broad swimmer's shoulders, narrow waist with a trail of blond hair leading down into his boxers. Strong legs, not too hairy. She wanted another glance at his boxers, but forced her eyes to his. Ice blue, staring. "I'm a nurse," she said, as though that were a full explanation of everything that was happening, the sudden flash of desire and the automatic denial of it. "I know what to do." *If I was wrong in yielding to persuasion once, remember that it was to persuasion exerted on the side of safety, not of risk.*

He raised his hands, mock surrender. A tiny smile. "I was only trying to help."

"I'm fine." She ran the cold water over her hand, examined the burn. It wasn't anything; she didn't even need a bandage. But she kept looking at it so that she wouldn't have to look at him. The omelet began to burn. Kevin moved to adjust the heat, and Janie snapped out of her examination. "Don't!" she said, reaching the skillet handle first. "I mean ... don't trouble yourself. I can take care of it."

Kevin wrinkled his eyes, made a moue of amusement. "Isa was right. You do have a mind of your own." Then he shrugged and went back into Isa's bedroom, not bothering to close the door as he dressed. A minute later, with his shoes hooked onto two fingers and his messenger bag slung over his shoulder, he returned. "Hope your hand's okay," he said.

Janie looked at him long enough to nod, vaguely, then turned back to the stove, her shoulders forward, her tired head down. She pretended to monitor the burned omelet until she heard the apartment door close behind her, waited a beat, and then threw the skillet into the sink, clatter and sizzle and bits of egg flying.

"Fuck you!" she yelled at the pan. She wanted to dump the whole mess onto the center of Isa's bed, right on the wet spot that Kevin had no doubt made, because it was so easy for Isa to gather a man into her life and bedroom and do with him what she wanted, and it had been years — years! — since Janie had been with a man, even though she longed for it more than almost anything. She lay nearly every morning in her sagging bed after her shower, after Isa and her balladeers had left, and she touched herself, thinking of Captain Wentworth, or sometimes Isa's spent men. Sometimes, when she finished, she cried. The depth of her loneliness was that great. Then she would wrap up in her robe, embarrassed even though nobody was there to see, and she would lose herself again between the pages of her favorite novel until she could move again and face the blank of another day.

The door closed behind Kevin and the smoke of burned eggs mingled with the steam of water on the skillet thrown into the sink and then there was the nasal honk of the fire alarm going off in the kitchen. "Goddamn it," Janie said, wrapping her robe tight, grabbing the broom to poke the off button on the disc mounted on the ceiling. Nothing. She went into the pantry and found the step stool, tried again, but still the alarm sounded. "Shut the fuck up," she hissed at the alarm as she poked, palms wet. There was nothing to do but to climb up onto the counter and pull it off, and so she hiked her robe up and pressed a knee onto the granite, which hurt, and wobbling, heaved herself up. She was dizzy at the height, the exertion and the adrenaline, and she reached up to twist the unit counter-clockwise off its base. She had to rise onto her toes to do so, fighting vertigo and imbalance, and just as she pulled out the batteries to stop the keening, the front door opened and Roscoe Jones, the superintendent, rushed in to see what was the matter.

He didn't even call her name. No "Miss-Janie-what's-the-matter" or anything of the sort. He rushed in, all six foot something, not saying a word, and he assessed the room, quickly, looking for the source. He saw the pan in the sink, checked the burners to make sure they were in the off position, glanced around the room at the outlets, lamps, television set. With nothing to claim his attention, he turned it to Janie, standing on the counter with the alarm in her hand and pissed-off panic on her face.

Roscoe offered her his hand. She took it and bent down, aware of herself and clutching her robe closed while she inelegantly worked herself off the counter.

"Thank you," she said. She lifted her sleeve to wipe the damp off her brow and then looked at the amputated alarm. She handed it to Roscoe, who accepted it as though it were a gift.

"Where's your phone?" he said. "You'll need to call the alarm company, let them know it's not an emergency so they can tell the dispatchers."

"Dispatchers?"

"The alarm," he said. "It signals the fire department automatically when it goes off."

"Oh."

He scanned the kitchen, found the phone, and dialed. "I need to report a false alarm." He gave the address and answered the operator's questions. "Kitchen." "Burned food." "Under control." "Brownie" was his response to the security question. "Sorry to trouble you," he said before he hung up.

"They'll show up anyway," he said. "Once they get called, you can't cancel."

Janie nodded. "Stupid me."

"Of course not," he said. "It can happen to anybody."

"But it would absolutely, obviously, irrefutably happen to me." And to her horror and possibly to his, she plunged her face in her hands and began to cry. Already, they could hear the sirens approaching.

"I need to go down and tell them where the alarm came from. They'll have to come up, just to check things out," he said. Then gently, "You might want to put on some clothes."

She looked down at herself and felt her face flash hot. Roscoe nodded once, looking at the floor, then went to lead the firefighters back up to her apartment, where the only thing burning was her cheeks.

It was quick and formal. Four sturdy men in bunker gear entered the apartment and looked around, asked her a few questions. After one of them entered his notes in a logbook, they filed out, solemn as they came. The one with the silver handlebar mustache stopped at the door and said to Roscoe, "Everything looks okay, but since we're here, we just have to check that the elevator's up to code. We'll let you know if we find anything, otherwise we'll just sign it off."

Roscoe nodded. He knew the elevator worked just fine. It had for as long as he could remember. He extended his four-fingered hand and the firefighter shook it. "Sorry for the bother," Roscoe said.

When they left, he turned to Janie. "Are you okay?" he asked.

She gave a half-smile and shrugged. There was the matter of the burned eggs, and her girth, and the disinterested looks on the firefighters' faces when they looked at her then past her, and Isa's naked men, and the rumbling in her stomach, which she would ignore as long as she could. There was a rumbling in some other part of her too, which she could not.

The whisper of her subconscious told her that while her humiliation felt unmitigated, there was still opportunity to reverse it — and it was standing directly in front of her, looking at her directly with eyes that had seen more than twice her years and who knows what else. But he didn't look away, even when she did, and when he spoke, his voice was calm as still water and it sounded to her lonesome ears as if he were speaking not to her but *into* her, and she closed her eyes for a moment, absorbing the echo of it. *Are you okay? Are you okay? Are you okay?* And when the memory of his voice grew faint, she opened her eyes and looked at him. They were only a few feet apart, his hands hung by his sides. He was tall and appeared strong, even with his history — however long it was — bearing down on him, pulling at his cheeks and eyes and shoulders. His eyes were a pale brown, almost metallic somehow, and as she stood looking up at him, a look of concern came to occupy his face. It was that look that made her do it; she didn't want him feeling sorry for her. She didn't want to always be the victim, the loser. She had something to offer someone. She did.

She closed the gap between them with one long step, then reached up with both her hands and pulled his face down to hers. She pressed her lips against his and held them there, and Roscoe sucked in a short breath of air through his nose. Not having had enough confidence or practice to know how best to proceed, she simply kept her lips against his and waited for him to take over. But he did not. Instead, his body seemed to stiffen, and his lips, which a moment ago had been full and generous, seemed to tighten against themselves as though he were trying to hold in that small gasp of air, or else keep her out. As she became aware of his rigid posture, it felt like they'd been standing there, lips together, for whole minutes. That brief, spontaneous unfurling of herself, that simultaneous offer of and demand for affection — which she might have looked back on as a pivotal moment in her evolution as a fully realized sexual being — was very, very quickly becoming the latest of her many regrets.

She knew she should just break the seal and let him go. Chuckle even, at her own impetuousness

— *How silly of me!* — and show him out, no hard feelings. But that was something Isa would do. No, Isa wouldn't do that; she wouldn't have to do that. Likely nobody had ever clamped his lips against a kiss from her. So with her bitterness rising and her humiliation not quite complete, Janie pointed her tongue and let it slide between her own lips and poked it at the impassable barrier of his. At this, Roscoe lifted his hands to her shoulders and pulled slowly away as though not to provoke the snake darting out at him. But it did provoke her, this slight rejection. All at once she saw Isa at her doorway and Kevin naked on her bed and she smelled the burned eggs and the endless banquet of donuts in the hospital break room and she heard the shriek of the fire alarm and the mournful wail of the fire truck coming to douse her flames, all the flames, until she had nothing. She was Anne Elliot, doomed to spinsterhood at age twenty-seven. But for her, there would be no Captain Wentworth to rescue her at the end.

And as Roscoe was pulling his face away from hers, she pulled it right back and quick as a snake, as a licking flame, she bit him on the lip.

"Jesus!" he said, yanking away. "What the hell

was that?" All the softness was gone. He touched his lip and pulled his hand away to check for blood. When he looked back at her, the shock on his face was far worse than if he'd been angry.

"Oh my god, I'm sorry," she said. Instinctively, she lifted a hand — the nurse in her — but he took a step back and shook his head.

"You bit my lip," he said. "My *lip*."

"I'm so sorry. I didn't mean —"

"How am I supposed to play my trumpet?" His face, open and astonished, looked like a child's.

"Oh god," she said, her hands against the weapon, her mouth. They stood there for a moment, looking at each other, letting the awareness settle in. For him, his injury; for her, her shame. *Are you okay? Are you okay?*

"No, god," she finally said, and ran for the door, bumping into an easy chair along her way. She recovered without stopping, and didn't close the door behind her.

Roscoe could hear her crying as she stood at the elevator, waiting and waiting for it to rescue her. But of course it did not; it was occupied while the firemen did their safety tests. He could tell by the fading sound of her crying that she had finally given up and left by way of the stairs.

His lip was fine after all. He iced it for a quarter of an hour and drank a cold beer. The next morning it was vaguely sore but not swollen, and the day after that he was able to play. With the exception of the memory, it was as though it had never happened.

Janie, on the other hand, was not so easily healed. Though maybe, hopefully, she eventually was. He wouldn't know. She fled her apartment that morning, as Roscoe regained his composure and the firefighters deemed the elevator up to code, and she never returned. He kept an eye out for her the first few days, then summoned the nerve to ask Isa about her, careful not to betray her any further.

"She's moving out," Isa said, and shrugged. "She sent me a letter and said she couldn't live with me anymore." She looked down and started to say something but stopped. "Anyway, she asked Trudy to pack up her stuff. She said she'd have somebody pick it up."

Falling now — actually, at this point, it felt more

like floating — nearly to the ledge of what had been her third floor window, Roscoe wondered what would have happened if he'd been the kind of man to allow an unwanted kiss. But he would never know, not even if he floated or fell for all of eternity, because he was not that kind of man.

2

It's been said that as people age, their ability to remember recent events can become compromised while their recall of things long past seems to sharpen. Forgotten moments return with such sudden clarity that any intervening passage of time seems to loop back onto itself until the memory abuts the present, so that, for example, a sixty-seven-year-old man on the outside of the building where he'd lived out his entire life could look inside, into the window of the second floor, and remember with absolute clarity the June afternoon of the year he turned seventeen, when the building manager was showing that empty corner apartment to a young married couple, Iris and Frank Montgomery.

Roscoe could remember precisely the slant of

light on the freshly sanded hardwood floor, the way the motes lit up as they floated languidly into the trapezoid of light, the drone of the manager enumerating the features of the apartment — the high ceilings, the spacious kitchen, the spare bedroom that could be turned into a nursery when the time came.

He could remember her, so young, only nineteen but trying to look older with her white gloves and patent leather handbag, standing with her shoulders back and her flipped-up blonde hair neat around her small ears, her arm looped through her husband's like she was trying to convince herself that she really was a married woman — the wife of a *doctor* — and not the university freshman she'd been just the year before. She kept glancing out the window, clinging to her husband's robust arm. A tumble off the roof of her childhood home when she was eight meant she would never be comfortable living anywhere higher than ground level.

"It seems awfully high up, doesn't it?" she said to nobody in particular.

"That's only because the ceilings in all the apartments are so high," the manager said. "Lots of extra space for a tall man." He looked at Frank and smiled. He was a good salesman, always appealing to the vanities of future tenants.

While the manager was pressing the sale, Iris looked at Roscoe, who was standing by the door with his four-fingered right hand shoved deep in his pocket, and fixed her stare on him long enough to make him uncomfortable. She looked desperate and pleading, skinny in her grown-up clothes. *Help me,* her hazel eyes seemed to say. *I don't want to fall.*

But then again, maybe his memory was playing tricks, distorting the order of things remembered, because he didn't know those things about her until later.

Roscoe, too, was young. He was shadowing the building manager because his father was sick and needed his son to grow up, fast. Roscoe had become a sort of informal apprentice to anyone who worked in the building. He earned no money, no praise from his father for his sacrifice, but learned everything he needed to about plumbing, electrical work, air conditioning, waste management. He learned how to accept deliveries and hold open doors. Because he was quiet, he observed that people who didn't need him for anything could walk past him without a glance in his direction. They would keep talking to their spouses or friends, or keep thinking their private thoughts, but he learned how to watch. He learned how to be invisible. This, his father told him, was the most important thing.

"Keep your head down, boy, and don't make no trouble. You just help them people out when need be and mind your own business. They ain't your friends," his father said just before he died. "You remember that."

But watching them all come and go, unstopping their toilets and changing their locks and listening to the private conversations they didn't even try to hide — how could he not think of them as something like friends? He could tell when someone was in trouble, or had difficulties of one type or another. He could tell their stories by the way they walked and the belongings they carried and their sighs or smiles when they collected the mail from their boxes.

He didn't have any friends of his own. When he wasn't working, he went out onto the roof and played his trumpet, trying to re-teach his fingers how to work the valves, trying not to think about what he no longer had. Nobody his own age understood what it was like to love music more than anything else, or what it felt like to lose a finger or a future. He didn't care about baseball or girls the way his classmates did. He was busy healing and hiding and learning how to be a superintendent so when his daddy died he could step in and take care of his mother, the way they both expected him to.

But something shifted that afternoon as the light crept slowly through the apartment and the manager was shaking Frank's hand and Iris was looking out the window with an expression that combined nausea and terror. Roscoe took a step toward them and said, more boldly than he ever would have imagined, "In case you don't like something about this one, I heard the one directly below this one will be coming up vacant soon. Mr. and Mrs. Kaufman are moving to California."

The manager looked at him, released Frank's hand and scratched the short, gray stubble on his chin. "Is that right?" he said. He'd just shaken hands on an easy deal. But Iris looked up at Roscoe and her lips parted just so, relief all over her face, the furrows across her brow smoothed down.

She turned to Frank. "Oh yes, dear, let's look at that one. This one's lovely, really, but I do think I'd prefer to be on the ground floor." She spoke quickly and the pink returned to her cheeks. Then she became aware of herself and added, "It'll be so much easier to manage, don't you think? With groceries and children and so forth?" After a moment, Frank reached out and cupped her face with his hand. He was only four years older than she, but with his broad back and square jaw and precise movements, he seemed old enough to be her father. He turned to the manager and shrugged.

"Let's take a look at that one then."

Iris took in a grateful breath of warm air, and let her eyes close. She told Roscoe later that she'd said a little prayer of thanks then, not to God but to him. But at the time, she'd only squeezed her husband's arm and nodded to the manager. Within four months, they'd signed the papers on the first floor apartment, made a substantial down payment courtesy of Frank's father, and moved themselves and their belongings in.

Roscoe's father died on a September afternoon the following year. Another loss to add to his accounts, but it wasn't the worst one on the list. He buried his father, looked after his mother, and kept on working full time as the building superintendent. The only thing that was different was that the checks that came every two weeks now were made out in his name, and he was offered a pension plan for which he had to choose a beneficiary. Since he had no wife, no children, and no prospects for either, he named his ailing mother as his heir.

He had seen Iris many times in the fifteen months after she and Frank moved in, but whatever bravado had moved him to speak that first time eluded him thereafter. She didn't seem to go out much, except for errands. She always returned carrying dry cleaning or grocery bags, occasionally shopping bags from Thrun's or Marshall Field's, and always when she saw him she smiled and waved a gloved hand if it happened to be available, and slowed down as though she might like to stop and talk. But her thin, ethereal beauty would make him falter, make him feel like he was falling down even if he were standing still. That translucent skin, those demanding blue veins that might as well have been pumping his own oxygen-depleted blood to her heart. That hollow at her throat, like an ongoing chorus straining at her neck. That smile, with the crease deeper on the one side, and the light shining in her pale eyes like a cherub's — no not that, like that of the girl, Paige, who'd beat him up every day after school for a year when they were ten. He'd let her do it, flailing her thin arms like windmills while they sweated over the cracked cement. He gave Paige a silver dove charm on her eleventh birthday with money he'd earned sweeping cigarette butts off the floor of the jazz club. That was his first and only girlfriend. Until Iris.

But Iris wasn't his girlfriend. She was a married woman, nearly twenty. Gloved and coiffed and smiling while he polished the banister or fixed the grill of the elevator — always keeping his hand out of the slam of it. He wanted to keep the nine fingers he had left.

Frank turned out not to be such an astute doctor after all. Who could be, really, at the age of twenty-three with only two years of college behind him before he undertook medical school? He said as much to his father, and then to Iris. Then one hot day, he walked the four blocks and enlisted as a medic before his swagger ran out.

Iris was devastated. Frank had saved her from loneliness when he met and married her. Her parents had died in an airplane crash when she was four, and she was sent to live with a spinster aunt she didn't know and who didn't want her. She wasn't abused, not outwardly. But she was often neglected, frequently ignored. She spent countless afternoons in her elementary school principal's office, not because she had misbehaved — she only misbehaved once in her entire life — but because her aunt had forgotten to pick her up. Eventually, the principal began to drive her home and she would wait in the empty house until her aunt returned, cutting out paper dolls in ever more elaborate patterns to pass the lonely time.

After Frank left for basic training at Fort Benning, Iris became even slighter. The sharp angles of her shoulder blades showed through her summer dresses, whose bright colors made a dramatic contrast to her dull expressions. By the time Frank had become a Spec-4 medic serving as doctor to the women and children of Tây Ninh, Iris was practically a recluse. When she passed through the lobby on an errand that could no longer be postponed, she looked only at the floor, or at her feet, as though her mobility required all of her attention. She hadn't waved to Roscoe in months.

Then there was an early December night when

the weather had turned wet and Iris came in carrying a paper sack of groceries. Roscoe was setting up the Christmas tree in the lobby, a job he performed with the same enthusiasm he had for changing locks or unclogging toilets, when she slipped and landed on her backside, her eyes wide and then, as nothing but soup cans rolled out of the split bag in ten directions, filling with tears. She hadn't seemed to notice Roscoe and, perhaps thinking she was alone, she made no move to stand. Instead, she leaned forward and drew up her knees and with her handbag still looped around one arm, pressed the heels of her hands to her eyes and cried.

Roscoe stepped out from behind the tree and gathered up the cans: onion and cream of asparagus and chicken noodle. He twisted the split end of the bag and put the cans inside, holding it like a baby so it wouldn't fall again. He tapped Iris gently on the shoulder and she looked up, surprised to see him and then embarrassed. She hurried off the floor and smoothed out her skirt. "I'm sorry," she started, but he just shook his head.

"I'll carry these for you," he said with a quiet inflection that almost curled his statement into a question. She seemed about to refuse, but almost immediately gave up on the idea of doing it herself.

"Thank you."

They walked side-by-side down the corridor to her apartment, not speaking. But because he was taller, he could steal glances at her without her noticing. His gaze kept returning to the exposed part of her neck just below her left ear where a port-wine birthmark spread upward from the pale recesses beneath, and he was gripped by the desire to unwind her scarf and peel off her clothes to see how far down it went.

She unlocked the door and he followed her inside. It was clean, calm, almost brutally spare. The lamps on either side of the low sofa were on, casting a glow around the living room. There seemed to be only what was needed and used. No silly corner hutches with bric-a-brac. No useless arrangements cluttering the space. But on every wall hung several art pieces—all variations on the same theme. They were single sheets of white paper from which something had been cut: flowers, skeletons, insects, people. From the very bottom of the negative space that represented the object, the scraps that had been cut away bent forward, becoming the object's shadow. Roscoe clutched the bag of soup cans and stared at a large one in which the shape of a tree silhouetted against the olive-green wall behind it loomed over its cutaway mirror image, which, after being folded down and manipulated, became its root system.

"I used to make paper dolls," she said by way of explanation. "When I was young."

Still holding the soup, he turned to her. "You still are."

"No. Not anymore," she said, looking down at the toes of her low-heeled boots. After a moment, she looked up at him. "Well, I'm not even sure I ever was."

He held her eyes as long as he could, feeling a heat rise up, then walked into the kitchen and started unpacking the broken bag. She followed him in and took the cans from him two at a time and stacked them in the pantry. He noticed that there wasn't much else there. "Maybe it's because you eat too much soup," he said, not quite under his breath, wishing immediately he hadn't.

Then she laughed. A snicker at first. A chortle. Then it snagged on itself and tumbled forward and grew into a great, deep belly laugh that rounded her sharp angles and infected Roscoe, who was susceptible with relief, until they were both clutching their middles and leaning on the kitchen table for support. By the time they wound down to catching their breaths, a space had opened up between them. She asked him to sit down at the table, and made him a cup of coffee. As he sipped it, she finished putting away the soup, chatting as she did so, seeming more robust just from having laughed, and he thought of his grandparents sharing a single cup of coffee, his grandmother perched on his grandfather's lap at the table, and he wished that Iris would walk over, unbidden, and do the same with him.

The next evening, he brought sandwiches from the Jewish deli and a bottle of table wine. When she answered the door, she was holding an X-ACTO knife. He raised his hands stick-up style. "I'll give you all my money," he said. She laughed again and opened the door wider to let him pass.

He hadn't gone there intending to woo her. He knew nothing of women or romance or seduction. The wine he brought was the first he'd ever tasted in all his almost nineteen years. He just wanted to be near her, to hear her laugh, to keep her safe if he could. From what, he didn't even know. He wanted to feed her and talk to her and watch her cut things out of paper, making negatives into positives, visibility from invisibility, all from the relative safety of the apartment on the ground floor.

The passage of time had slowed considerably as Roscoe fell. All around him, he could see particles in the air, the dust and soot and pollen, the water molecules from Lake Michigan, reflecting light in all directions. The window of the second floor glowed pink and orange as he looked at it. His memories, too, hung in the air around him. Molecules of time, floating around him, keeping him buoyed. It seemed as though he weren't even falling anymore. There were groans coming from somewhere, low growls of a dog barking or a taxi honking, like a 45-rpm record being played at 33-rpm. He looked through the glare of the second floor window and remembered.

They had become the very best of friends, he and Iris, after just a month or so. It became routine for them to eat dinner together and afterward, play cards or watch The Dick Van Dyke Show or something else on television. Sometimes she would work on one of her art pieces, and he might clean his trumpet while she cut, watching the intent look on her face as she did so. He never overstayed; at her first yawn he would stand and begin to tidy up, even as she protested, and they would say good-night without so much as a handshake. As the months wore on and the Kennedy administration increased the U.S. military participation in Vietnam and bits of green began to burst from underneath the melting snow, Roscoe and Iris settled into their own form of domestic harmony.

One night, he was playing a song for her, at her request. She was leaning into the corner of the angular couch, her knees drawn up beneath a throw, a half-drunk cup of coffee at her elbow. It was her favorite, the one she always asked for. "Yesterdays." His fingers were still adapting to the loss of one of their own, the new arrangement still uncertain on the valves. But with Iris watching, Roscoe didn't mind. He closed his eyes and buzzed his lips and found that perfect blue note that would set them off on a melancholy journey, apart but together, starting and ending in Iris's living room but traveling the history of the world in between. That night, when he stopped, she didn't offer her soft applause the way she usually did. This time, she was crying.

He put down his Blessing and walked over to her, sat on the edge of the couch. He reached out and smoothed her hair, and his fingers tingled at the softness of it. She looked up at him finally and said, "I just miss him so much."

Roscoe withdrew his hand like it had been burned.

"Don't," she said, and reached for it. She closed her eyes and pressed his palm against her face, cupping it the way Frank had done that day when they were looking at the second floor apartment, except his had only the four fingers. For the first time since it had happened, he was glad his middle finger was gone. If he'd had all five, he might have gone to Vietnam. He might have been patrolling the periphery, trying to intercept forces from North Vietnam. He might have been lying somewhere, wounded by a mortar attack, getting an IV or a tourniquet from Frank instead of sitting on Frank's couch, cupping his wife's perfect face with his imperfect hand.

Before he knew what was happening, they were kissing, slowly at first then clutching at each other, pulling off their clothes, him pushing her hair off her face, damp with tears and heat, her pulling him to the bedroom, pulling him onto her, into her.

It didn't last long — certainly not long enough for him. Not even now, with time slowed to 33-rpm. He wished he could go back and do it all over again, and again. That was the one and only time he ever made love to Iris, or to anyone.

She fell asleep in his arms and he lay awake looking at her for an hour or more, not wanting to move even when his limbs went numb and needled. Squinting in the dark, he memorized the shape of the port-wine birthmark that started below her left ear and went down to her clavicle. She woke slowly, looked at him strangely for a moment, then pushed herself up and sat on the edge of the bed with the sheet wrapped around her. "Roscoe ..." she started, not looking at him.

She was looking at one of her cutouts hanging on the bedroom wall. It was of two people, a man and a woman standing apart, not touching. But their cutaway shadows had been shaped so that it looked like they were holding hands.

Roscoe wanted to reach out and pull her back, to slow down time so that she was still asleep in his arms, or better, still beneath him, making love.

But he only touched the sheet where she had been, which was cooling already, and said, "I understand."

He pressed himself up out of the bed, and his limbs ached where they'd fallen asleep. He felt simultaneously like an old man and a child. He gathered his clothes, groping in the dark, and as he was about to leave, she whispered, "I love you."

"I love you, too," he said into the shadows. Then he showed himself out, guiding the door without watching it until he heard the click, quiet as a kiss, behind him.

Frank returned a few months later with a silver star and a shattered arm. He was wounded in other ways that no one would ever know, but Roscoe could see the haunted look in his eyes. Frank spent a great deal of time shuttered inside the apartment on the ground floor while Iris tended to him however she did. Eventually, Frank returned to his residency program, choosing psychiatry as his specialty. Iris may or may not have continued her paper arts; he no longer visited her apartment. Even when they needed something repaired, she didn't ask him to do it. Yet whenever they happened to pass each other, she would look at him, briefly, and smile before continuing on her way.

Roscoe started a rumor in 1964 that continued for the next forty-seven years, and possibly would keep going even long after he was gone. He said that the apartment on the second floor, the one directly above Iris's, was haunted. That he'd seen the ghost himself, a young man of about nineteen or twenty who'd died of a broken heart and wandered the apartment looking for his lost love. The tenants who occupied that apartment didn't stay long the way people in the other apartments did. They would move in and then someone would tell them about the haunting. Their sleep would become disturbed and they would add new reports to the rumor, and eventually they would move on. When their things were gone and the apartment was empty again, Roscoe would take his time preparing it for the next sale. He would wash and paint and make repairs and all the other normal things. But he would also always refinish the floors, even if they didn't need it. He would sand through the old finish down to the oak, a dust-producing, time-consuming process.

And always, before he applied a new coat of polyurethane, while the wood was still bare, he would lie down on the spot that would be directly above her bed and press his ear to her ceiling, one eighth of an inch closer to her than the last time, listening to the sound of his own heart beating.

1

Iris became ill a few months before Roscoe began his fall. It was the middle of summer when he first noticed it. There had already been more than twenty consecutive days of record heat, but when she passed through the lobby carrying a plastic bag of groceries, looking pale and thinner than usual, she wore a sweater.

He climbed down from the ladder and pocketed a light bulb. He stepped quietly into her path as though it were fifty years ago. "Let me carry that for you."

She stopped, and smiled as she always did. "I'm fine. It's nothing." The plastic rattled in her grip. Normally he would have nodded and let her pass without pressing her further, but this time he stood where he was and searched her face.

"You've got a fever." He wanted to kiss her forehead to be sure, the way his mother had when he was a child. He wanted to take her home and tuck her into bed and smooth back her hair, which had gone gradually white over the years.

"I'm just a little tired," she said, and smiled again. "It's nothing."

It wasn't nothing, he could tell. He knew her as well as he knew their building, as well as he knew himself. He'd watched the years pull on her, humping her back and turning her blue veins ropy beneath her translucent skin. Her knuckles gnarled and her waist, which had never distended with a child, finally thickened with age. There was a deep spray of lines that fanned away from her eyes, but to him it was like looking at rays of the sun.

He could have left the building years ago. Decades ago. He could have left Chicago altogether, caught a train or a boat bound for elsewhere, found a girl, made a family. But he didn't. As long as Iris was there, even if she were living happily ever after with another man, he knew he wouldn't leave.

The sun had begun to set by the time he began his fall some seconds before, and the colors whorled around him in their improbable blends: pink-orange and purple-gray. He reached out, slowly, languid, feeling the air pass between his nine fingers, slowing him down until he felt like he was barely moving. He dropped gently as a falling leaf, resistant to the wind. He felt light as one, too, as though some amount of weight were jettisoned with each memory recalled and remembered. All those experiences had mass; some, of course, had more than others.

As he hovered past the lintel of the window of the first floor apartment, he reached out and put his palm against the glass. But he didn't care to look inside. That wasn't where he would find her.

Roscoe had gone to bed early the night the ambulance came. He'd played his trumpet for a while, feeling the ache of all his sixty-seven years in his fingers, even the missing one. Then he'd had a beer and read for a while, Castro's copy of *Mrs. Dalloway.* It was as warm and quiet as a cocoon inside his apartment, and he turned on the old metal fan as much to camouflage the silence as to move the air. He fell into a light sleep, and when the sirens screamed at the front of the building, he incorporated them into the dream he was having, turning it into the sound that used to accompany that colorful test pattern on television after a station went off-air for the night. He didn't learn that Iris had been taken away until three days later.

A stout man in his forties carrying a paper cup of coffee knocked on Roscoe's door and introduced himself as Frank and Iris Montgomery's nephew, Alan, and asked if Roscoe would let him into their apartment with the master key.

Roscoe hesitated, trying to remember Alan, unsure if he was indeed one of the members of Iris's family who'd visited them throughout the years. He was about to say no, he was sorry, but he couldn't let anyone into a tenant's apartment without permission, but Alan said, "My uncle's inside. He's just confused, I think. I went to get a decent cup of coffee down the street, but I left my keys inside. I was pre-caffeinated, you know what I mean?" He laughed at his own joke.

"Is Iris — Mrs. Montgomery — home?"

"Oh, you didn't know?" He tilted his head like a puppy. "Well, why would you, I guess —"

"Know what?" Roscoe stepped out into the hall.

"My aunt's in the hospital. My uncle —"

"Which hospital?" He was already reaching for his jacket.

"Memorial. But — are you friends?"

Roscoe didn't answer, just found his own key on the ring and locked his apartment door. "Come on," he told Alan. "I'll open your aunt's apartment for you."

Alan prattled on as he tried to keep up with Roscoe's longer strides, holding a hand over his coffee to keep it from spilling. "My uncle's not doing too well without Aunt Iris. He was already a little absentminded, forgetting people's names, telling stories about people nobody's heard of, thinking it was Friday when it was Monday and so forth. It's been getting bad for a while, actually." He jogged a few steps to catch up. "I don't know what I'm going to do if Aunt Iris doesn't get better soon. It's just me. I'm the only family they've got left, but I've got my two girls back in Minnesota with their mom. I can't stay here indefinitely, you know?"

Alan's voice became white noise. Roscoe kept thinking of Iris sitting in the middle of the lobby in 1961, two dozen cans of soup rolling around the marble floor. Then just that week, looking so frail.

He should have talked to Frank. He should have insisted on something.

At the Montgomery apartment, Roscoe knocked once, then again more loudly, then opened the door with the master key. Alan went in and hurried to the bedroom. Roscoe stepped inside and looked around. The furniture was mostly the same, stylish again after so many years. There were other changes; a different rug, new paint, evidences of an elderly life: boxes of tissues, Frank's cane, a tray of prescription bottles on the lamp table next to a worn-in easy chair. But there were the paper cutouts, still framed and hung on all the walls. He closed his eyes and took a breath. The room still smelled the same.

"He's fine," Alan said, startling Roscoe back to present day. "Just fell asleep."

Roscoe nodded and turned to go. "Take care," he said. Before Alan could respond, Roscoe had already closed the door and was walking fast toward the lobby, hoping there'd be a taxi just outside.

The volunteer at the information desk told him what floor she was on, and to check in at the nurses' station. He hurried through the halls, following signs, up the elevator, all along passing solemn visitors and bewildered children and overpriced stuffed animals from the hospital gift store and patients dragging IV stands. He had a sudden memory of being in the emergency room at this same hospital, his hand wrapped in one of his mother's kitchen towels, his father pale beside him, saying, "You a fool, boy. Always got your head somewhere else. You ain't careful, you going to keep losing bits of yourself one at a time 'til there's nothing left."

He got to the nurses' station and put all nine fingers on the counter. "I'm looking for Iris Montgomery."

A thin nurse in purple scrubs looked at him over the rims of her glasses. "Are you a relation?"

Roscoe looked down at his hands, dark and gnarled. He remembered the way he'd threaded them through Iris's blonde hair before he kissed her that first time. "Distant," he said.

She moved a clipboard toward him. "Room 674. Sign here, please."

He knocked lightly, waited. He pressed the handle and let himself inside. After a lifetime of deference to other people's space, he always entered a room with a sense of trespass even when he was bidden. It was much more acute when he was not.

"Iris?"

She was asleep, pale and shrunken. An IV dripped clear liquid into a vein in her hand, which lay on top of the blue blanket that covered her. The television was on, something with one of those annoying laugh tracks. He found the remote and turned it off. He wished he'd brought flowers.

"Iris."

He lifted a chair and moved it to the side of her bed. He reached out and touched her hand, the one without the IV, then withdrew it. She didn't move. So he picked her hand up and laid it into his open palm, and one by one, ran his finger along the length of each of hers.

He never thought he would touch her again. All those years, all those nights he spent alone, hoping. Every time there was a knock at his door, every time the phone rang, part of him lit up, wanting it to be her. *I've left Frank.* Or *Frank left me.* Or *I can't stand it anymore, not being with you.*

I love you. I want you. I need you.

But nobody ever knocked or called who didn't need him for something other than love. They didn't need him to keep them company while they cut strange silhouettes out of paper, or to collect their errant soup cans from the foyer floor, or to make love to them because they loved him. They only ever needed him to be the superintendent. And that is what he was. And that is what he did, losing little bits of himself along the way.

The air around him was so thickly dense with particulates that it caught in the hair on his outstretched arms. Dust and soot, smoke and dirt consorted with nitrogen and oxygen and the noble argon and glittered in the setting October sun. All the years he had tended the building and its tenants, the wreckage of humanity was something to be discarded. But here it was, now, buoying him up.

A bird flew by, flapping its wings so slowly it seemed to be going backward. He thought again of Martin Delpy, naked and flapping his wings on the ledge of the fifth floor and his mother singing him in: *Bye, bye blackbird.* He lifted a finger and the bird hummed toward it. It was so close Roscoe could stroke its neck. If birds could smile, then this one did, giving him its full attention before it drifted upward, or Roscoe drifted downward. It was like plunging through molasses, but it didn't seem to matter. He could barely feel his own limbs by now.

"Roscoe?" she said. "Is that you there?" The monitors beeped responses to Iris's vital signs: cardiac and respiratory and hemodynamic. Roscoe had fallen asleep holding her hand, his head on his forearm. The beeping continued until he woke. He wiped his mouth on his shoulder, smacked away the sleep. The pins-and-needles sensation burned; he could barely feel his arm, but he didn't want to release her hand to shake it off. He would let it tingle to nothingness before he let her go.

"Yes," he said. "I'm here."

But she didn't respond. After a minute or so, he wondered if he'd only dreamed her voice. Her face was still, eyes closed, pale.

"Can you hear me, Iris?"

Her hand inside his was cool and dry. The intermittent beeping continued, but otherwise the only other noise was the din of the hospital beyond her room. Iris didn't move, and she didn't speak again — if she had spoken at all.

Does it ever get any fucking easier?

Roscoe turned in the air, slow, slow, like a wind-up toy whose potential energy is nearly expended as the rubber band unwinds its final rotation, and he saw the naked form of Lenny Dreyfus.

"Is that you, Narcissus?"

"Yes, Mr. Dreyfus."

"I'm Goldmund, remember? And look at you, still the ascetic." Lenny rolled onto his back and crossed one thin leg over the other, comfortable on some unseen cloud. "It does, you know."

"What's that?"

"It gets a lot fucking easier."

Roscoe stayed with Iris until the nurses made him leave, and then he returned the next day, and the next. In between, he invented a reason to visit Frank Montgomery at their apartment — an inspection for insects — and Frank answered the door wearing pajama pants and a suit jacket. When Roscoe explained his errand, Frank said, "Yes, of course, come in. I was just telling my wife we had something of an infestation going in the bedroom. Exceptionally large spiders. Big as my hand. And roaches, too, I think." He turned to the bedroom and called out. "Iris? Are you decent? The man from the fumigation company is here."

"Uncle Frank? Uncle Frank, who's there?" The toilet flushed and Alan emerged from the bathroom. "Oh, Mr. Jones — it's Mr. Jones, right? I'm sorry. Here, Uncle Frank. Come."

"I've just got to run down to the bank. You watch the fumigation man. I think he may be the one who's stolen from us before."

Alan blushed and made an apologetic face at Roscoe, then guided Frank back to the bedroom. Alan murmured to his uncle, low and soothing, then closed the door and returned.

"He's getting bad. I'm going to have to do something."

"Anything I can do?"

"I don't know," he said. "I'm taking it a day at a time."

"*Mira lo que veo en el cielo,*" said a deep and mellow voice nearby. Roscoe turned again, with so little effort, but so slowly, and beheld a wonderful surprise: his friend Joaquin. Roscoe noticed that he looked very trim, and considerably younger than he had at the time of his death. He had all his hair, as well as both of his feet. "Shall I read to you, my old friend? I find that *Don Quixote* is a good companion on a journey such as yours."

Roscoe smiled. Joaquin cleared his throat and began.

Here lies a gentleman bold
Who was so very brave
He went to lengths untold,
And on the brink of the grave
Death had on him no hold.
By the world he set small store--
He frightened it to the core--
Yet somehow, by Fate's plan,
Though he'd lived a crazy man,
When he died he was sane once more.

The nurse was putting something into the IV drip when Roscoe returned. "Her temperature's up," she said. "Maybe best if you don't stay too long." Roscoe lifted the chair and moved it next to Iris. He picked up her hand, the one without the needle, and it was warm.

"Come back, Iris," he whispered. "Come back to me." It was bold of him to ask, he knew, but what did he have left to lose? He'd never asked her for anything in all those years. He wouldn't now if he hadn't seen Frank. He wouldn't ask her to leave him of course, not completely. But maybe share a small part of the rest of her life. It could be simply lunch. Even just lunch once and a while would be something. It would be more than what he had.

He looked around at the people on the ground. The ones who had been listening to him play just a couple of seconds before. They seemed frozen, all of them, their mouths slack as they gripped their baby strollers or grocery sacks or paper cups of coffee. He wondered if Einstein had ever fallen off a building. It seemed to take so long to get to the ground, like time just got up and walked away. But even now, he could hear the faint last melodic phrase of "Yesterdays" that had come off his trumpet; those notes, a cascade of tenderness and pain, reassembled in his ears. He could feel his trumpet against his lips, Brownie's old Blessing that he'd never considered replacing. Since the day he'd first set eyes on her, he had called his trumpet Iris. And when he played, he played for her. It was the closest thing he had to her kiss.

"Come back to me, Iris," he said again. "The world's a lonely enough place already." He held her hand, feeling the heat come off her palm into his. This was the hand that had held his against her face that night. This was the hand that cut mysteries out of paper, that pulled soup cans off of shelves. This was the hand that he wanted to ask for. "Iris," he whispered. "Come back."

Her breathing changed. It was shallower and faster, like she wasn't getting enough air.

"Nurse?" Roscoe called. He looked up at the monitors, not understanding the waves and sounds, but the fact that everything seemed to speed up was alarm enough. "Nurse!"

He could feel her slipping away, though he couldn't have said why. They'd said that she was improving, that the infection was subsiding, but he knew. He wanted to lean over the bed and blow air into her lungs if she couldn't get enough on her own. He wanted to gather her up in his arms and take her home, carry her over the threshold and set her down on his lap for a cup of morning coffee. In that moment, he'd have gladly given up any of his other fingers just to have her back.

The nurse rushed in. "Did something happen? Did you see?" She checked the monitors and applied an oxygen mask. She pressed the call button and said to the other nurse, "Get a doctor."

Roscoe stood helpless against the wall as they moved around her, pushing medications, yanking open her gown for the paddles, all of them responding to the doctor's sharp commands. He held his breath — if she couldn't breathe, neither would he — trying to see her through their blurry huddle.

And then he could.

They buried her on a sunny morning in early October, in a plot that faced the lake. Alan was there with his ex-wife and daughters, a handful of friends, and Frank, who said after it was over, "Well done, Pastor. I'll be sure to tell Iris about it. She'll be sorry she missed it, I'm sure." If anyone thought it strange that the building superintendent was present, they didn't mention it.

The following week, Roscoe helped Alan pack up the contents of the Montgomery apartment. He thought about taking one of Iris's cutouts, but there was no reason to. He didn't need anything to remind him of her.

They moved Frank into a memory care facility, Alan guiding his uncle by the arm, Roscoe carrying his bags. When they walked through the lobby, a woman in a purple visor was screaming to her aide, "I need to go home! I want to go home! My husband needs his lunch cooked!" The aide wheeled her down the hall, but they could still hear her. "I need to kiss my husband his good morning!"

Roscoe shook hands with Alan first, and then Frank. "Take care, Mr. Montgomery."

Frank shook his hand, and looked him in the eye. "I'll do that," he said.

Roscoe went home, but before he went inside, he walked the block around the building. When he got to the uneven seam near the corner, he bent down and passed his hand over the weeds that grew between the buckled slabs. Then he went inside to his apartment and made himself a grilled cheese with tomato soup. He spent a good, long time cleaning his trumpet, then he went up onto the roof to play.

Yesterdays, yesterdays
Days are new as happy sweet
Sequestered days

Olden days, golden days
Days of mad romance and love

He slowed the tempo and approached the final note in the last melodic phrase. Just before he bowed he thought, *Iris, come back to me.*

He fell and fell. And now, there she was. She floated toward him, nineteen again, smiling. "I'm not afraid of falling anymore," she said.

He reached out to touch her and he could feel the smooth of her skin, but he couldn't feel his own — he was weightless now. He pulled her close through the glitter air, somewhere in the window span above the sidewalk, within the zoetrope of memory and flesh. When he held her smiling face with his gossamer hands, all ten fingers were there.

Just before his Blessing shattered against the broken sidewalk beneath them, she leaned into him and kissed him on the lips.

ACKNOWLEDGEMENTS

I want to thank those who provided information, insight, encouragement, enthusiasm, feedback, friendship, or love (and in some cases, all of it) during the creation of this book.

My thanks to my sushi-loving writing partner, David Eagleman, for encouraging the germ of this story, and for sharing his knowledge of time perception and the flexibility of memory. I'm deeply grateful to my old pal Ulises Larramendi and his father, Lincoln Larramendi, for sharing their memories of Cuba and their exile from the country they loved; they breathed life into Joaquin. I'm grateful to Dr. Tom Parr for our conversation about Vietnam. Thanks also to Mark McGinty, author of *The Cigar Maker*, for his descriptions of the daily life of *los lectores*. Many thanks go to Terry Love, the Seattle-based plumber who told me how to clog a toilet. Thanks to trumpeter Denis Dotson, who explained the basics of trumpet playing as well as the challenges a trumpeter would confront if he were to lose his middle finger. My deep gratitude also goes to Andrew Lienhard for his long friendship, his music, and for teaching me about fake books. Thanks to my friend Jon Kooker for scouting the historic Chicago building after which I modeled Roscoe's. Thank you to Janette Hearne for our wonderful conversations and for loaning me the line "time walked away from me." My warmest thanks go to Charlie Baxter for his friendship these many years and for the gift of a perfect ending.

For her unflagging faith in me, I am grateful to my agent, Jane Gelfman. Thanks go to Jesse Steele for her editorial scrutiny and her poetic insight. My profound love and gratitude go to my sister, Sara Huffman — the Poto to my Cabengo. Without her, my thoughts would have no anchors. Many, many thanks to my early readers, those cherished friends, especially to my script-writing partners Tobey Forney and Sarah Blutt; to Lee Ann Grimes, who always has a solution; and to Holly Wimberley, who has always believed. I send thanks to Mark Love, artist and thinker; his influence is reflected on these pages. I am deeply grateful for the love and support of my parents Cindy Slator and Larry Pullen — my first teachers and my biggest fans. Finally, I thank my husband Harris for enabling and encouraging my writer's life, for — along with our children Sasha and Joshua — forgiving the endless hours I spend at my desk, and for reminding me always of the real definition of success. For that and more, I love you.

The following books were invaluable to my research: *An Introduction to Metaphysics* by Henri Bergson, *Reminiscences of a Lector: Cuban Cigar Workers in Tampa* by Louis A. Pérez, Jr., *Narcissus and Goldmund* by Hermann Hesse, and *Hard Times: An Oral History of the Great Depression* by Studs Terkel.

CPSIA information can be obtained at www.ICGtesting.com
Printed in the USA
LVOW08s2223181213

365961LV00004B/309/P